AFTER HALASTAESIA

JANINA FRANCK

Snowy
Wings
PUBLISHING

AFTER HALASTAESIA

First Edition

Copyright @ 2024 by Janina Franck
www.janinafranck.com

Published by Snowy Wings Publishing,
PO Box 1035, Turner, OR 97392, USA
www.SnowyWingsPublishing.com

Cover art: Ali Lawson
Website: bookcoverdesign.alilawson.com

Editor: There For You Editing
Website: thereforyouediting.wordpress.com

ISBN (e-book): 978-1-958051-74-0
ISBN (paperback): 978-1-958051-75-7

For you.

PART I

CHAPTER 1

I didn't particularly enjoy the sticky feeling of the leathery couch on my skin, even if it was just on my arms. The smell was probably comforting to most people, but it reminded me of my grandparents' house from when I'd been young—cold and distant. Suffice to say, it wasn't exactly putting me at ease.

Still, Mom was right. I needed to talk about it with someone. I'd wanted that person to be her, or at least Harvey or Jack, but all of them only sighed whenever I brought up the subject.

"Look, man," Jack had said. "You've been through something really traumatic or whatever. But, like, you gotta see someone about this. It's not healthy."

Mom had agreed.

So I'd come to this stranger's office to talk about my experience, my adventure, my *fight*.

Now all I could think about was how I wanted to go back. Back to see Tara again, to joke around with Ronan, and to argue with Phillip. I still saw them sometimes, in my dreams, but that was different. It wasn't real. Then again, no one else believed they'd ever been real to begin with.

"So, Benjamin," the woman in the chair said, brushing a stray strand of her black hair out of her face.

"Just Ben is fine," I interrupted, hands kneading my jeans.

She nodded, adjusting her red-rimmed glasses. "Ben. Your mother has touched on a few points over the phone, but I'd like to hear it come from you. What is it that's bothering you?"

I glanced at her, in her black pencil skirt and pristine white blouse. I hadn't expected her to ask such a forward question. Was that normal? Since it was my first time seeing a therapist, I was severely lacking in reference points.

"I'm having trouble adjusting to being back," I said. "I was away for a little while, but now I'm back and it's … hard."

She scribbled some notes onto her little pad, and I surreptitiously glanced around the room. Overall, it gave me the distinct feeling of a living room, but more so a display living room than the kind people actually used. The table had no rings from glasses being put down without coasters, and an empty vase with a floral pattern occupied some space on the shelf flanked by books. A basket of squishy, brightly colored toys beside the beige leather couch drew my eye, and

I wondered if I was meant to take one of them. To me, they looked like chew toys for a dog.

My gaze returned to my new psychiatrist. A diploma on the wall identified her as Dr. Marilyn Steinberg. Based on her name, I wondered if she had German heritage. Would she try to explain everything away using Freud somehow? That seemed to be a common trend, if media was to be believed.

"And where is it you were?"

I gulped at her question. I hated this part. Still, it was best to just come right out and say it. After all, she couldn't help me if I didn't talk about what had happened. "I was saving another world."

"What was this world exactly? Can you describe it?"

I hesitated. How did you sum up an entire world? It wasn't like I'd gotten to see it all. I'd only traveled through a fraction of it, to gather allies and the magical artifacts to defeat the Corrupted Ones.

"It was a world of magic," I said. "Magic that comes from nature. So most of it was covered in trees, and lakes, and an ocean and mountains. Kind of like Earth, but wilder, and with less people. There were other races, too. Elves, and trolls, and dragons. My girlfriend, Tara, she's fae and …" I trailed off.

Thinking of Tara hurt. I might never see her again, and after everything we'd been through

… it wasn't easy to accept. I'd tried to figure out how to get back there, and I'd come up empty. But that was why I was here, wasn't it? To learn to accept that my life *there* was over.

"I see," Dr. Steinberg said. "And how did you get to this world?"

My fingers fidgeting, I bit the inside of my cheek. This was the bit that everyone always put so much emphasis on, wasn't it? The part that made everyone say that it was all just a dream.

"There was an accident." Pausing, I twisted my head to watch her watching me. Her expression was one of keen listening and she waited patiently for me to continue. I turned my head back to look at an abstract painting hanging on the wall. I was half certain that it was a Picasso print. "I was cycling to my friend's house after school, near the fairgrounds at the edge of town, but there was ice on the road. There was a truck and neither of us could brake properly. I got hit, and fell into a coma."

These were the facts. I remembered getting hit by the truck, but it had happened so fast, I'd never even felt the impact. I'd seen it racing toward me, and the next thing I'd known, I'd woken up in a field of wildflowers, with two imps running toward me yelling something about the Chosen Hero having finally arrived.

I gulped, waiting for what Dr. Steinberg would say.

"What you're saying is that the act of falling

into a coma transported you into this other world?"

I nodded and shrugged at the same time. Putting it that way didn't feel entirely right, but it certainly wasn't entirely wrong, either. It wasn't like I had any other theories.

"And how did you manage to return to *this* world?"

"It wasn't by choice," I blurted out. Taking a deep breath, I counted to five before continuing more calmly. "The silver-banded mages decided that, as an outsider, I could not be allowed to remain in Halastaesia, so they thanked me for my service and cast a spell to send me home. That's when I woke up in the hospital."

Some more scribbling. Even though I wasn't watching, I could hear the scratching as the pen danced across the paper. I waited for the next question, certain I wouldn't like it.

"How much time did you spend in … Halstisia, was it?"

"Halastaesia," I corrected her. "I was there for twelve months, nine days, and twelve hours."

"And how long were you in a coma?"

I'd been right. I didn't like the question.

"Three months, two days, and nine hours," I recited. "Give or take a few minutes."

More scribbling.

"Why did you not want to come home?"

"Are you kidding me?" I threw my hands up in the air. "Everything was perfect … the bad guys were defeated, I was a *hero,* and everyone loved me. I had the coolest friends in the world that I'd gone through hell with, and I even got the girl. It's everything I ever wanted! And then it was taken from me."

I'd almost started yelling.

The sound of furious scribbling made me sink back into myself.

"Tell me about your relationships with the people in your life on Earth. Let's start with your mother."

Didn't I freaking know it?

Mom glanced at me sideways. Even without looking back at her, I knew that she was giving me that sympathetic smile. She knew this was hard for me, but she didn't understand why. *Couldn't* understand why. No one on this damned planet could know what I was going through.

"How was it?" she asked.

I shrugged, resting my chin in my hand as I stared out of the car's side window. "Fine."

Truthfully, I felt like I'd been forcing myself to remember all the painful parts of being back, and I didn't really see how therapy could help me.

Mom reached out to me and stroked my cheek.

"Honey, it'll get easier. I promise. You just have to give it some time. You're back in school next week, won't that be something?"

School. It seemed so trivial compared to everything I'd gone through. I'd fought literal monsters in life-or-death battles, had outwitted a millennia-old tree, and tamed a Lovecraftian creature from the deepest crevices of Halastaesia. But yes. In this world I still had to go to *school*.

"Sure."

Sighing sadly, she turned on the car.

I really was sorry to give her pain, and it wasn't like I hadn't sometimes missed her when I'd been in Halastaesia, but I'd felt like I belonged there. I'd been special.

She didn't understand what it felt like, going from being truly exceptional to being a nobody—just another kid in high school. Their problems seemed so trivial to me, so juvenile. Teenagers complaining about homework? Give me a break. Try battling a cyclops with nothing but a dagger, and then we'll see which you'd prefer.

And it was *because* Mom couldn't understand that I couldn't open up to her anymore. I'd tried. I'd seen the pitying look she'd given me. The doctors had explained that coma dreams can sometimes feel just as real as reality, and that it might take a while for me to figure out the difference between dream and real life.

Except, based on the things I'd read on the internet, the way that usually worked was that a person would start second guessing whether they were even awake, or whether they were still in the dream. That wasn't the case for me. I knew that I was awake, that this was real. What made me so miserable was that I knew my time Halastaesia had been real, too.

Mom parked the car in our driveway, and I headed straight to my room.

"Dinner'll be ready soon!" she yelled after me.

"'Kay."

I'd join her for the meal, if only to keep her from eating alone, but I hadn't had any appetite since coming back. Sure, the scratchiness of my throat the first few days hadn't helped, but even after it healed, I'd had to force myself to eat.

After stalking through the scattered clothes on my bedroom floor, I went to my bedside table and pulled open the top drawer. The ring on the chain was still there.

Any time I started doubting for even a second if my memories were real, I just needed to look at it, to feel it. I sighed in relief as I put it back around my neck, where it belonged. Tara had given it to me.

It was the only tangible proof I had left of my time in Halastaesia, and it had still been in my hand when I'd awoken in the hospital room. Mom thought that someone visiting must have left it for me, probably another get-well gift, like the fruit baskets and the flower arrangements, but I knew the truth. After all, the inscription on the inside in Tara's language was still there—*I love you*.

Though I supposed to anyone else it just looked like another weird squiggle.

Deciding to let out some of my pent-up frustration, I climbed down into the basement, put on my noise-canceling ear protectors, and worked away on my drum set. I really went to town on them, striking every drum with just the right amount of force, keeping rhythm, but slowly going faster and faster, until my ears could barely distinguish the sounds anymore.

By the time I was done, I was panting, and my ears were ringing despite the mufflers, but I felt better. Well enough to even bless my Mom with some smiles while we were having dinner and chatting away.

I was grateful she didn't try to bring up the therapy session again. Instead, she focused on my return to school. It was nearing the end of March now, my accident having taken place at the start of December. There were only three months of school left, but she was hoping that was enough time for me to catch up with my studies, if I was up for it, so I could advance into the next year along with the rest of my peers.

I couldn't care less.

But it mattered to her, so I nodded and smiled, saying I would do my best.

Mr. Smith had already sent over my timetable for this semester, so I was able to prepare just fine.

"Hun, what would you like for dinner tomorrow?" Mom asked as she cleared the table.

"A stew might be nice," I said, and a flash of joy crossed her face. I wasn't entirely surprised. That may have been the first time I actually requested a dish since coming back. The truth was, I missed stews. I'd eaten a lot of them in Halastaesia, and while it wasn't going to be similar in any shape or form, it was as close to something from there as I could get here.

"I'll make sure it's the best stew you've ever had," Mom promised.

I forced a smile, knowing that even with all her prowess in the kitchen, that was a promise she couldn't keep.

I helped her with the dishes, something I used to avoid like the plague. When I was done, I hugged her and gave her a kiss on the cheek, something that I also never used to do and would be teased about if anyone my age in this world saw. But hey, life-changing adventures in a different world can have that effect on a guy. It was my way of apologizing for making her worry. And I knew she'd worried a lot ... still did. And my sulkiness certainly wasn't helping.

My awareness of my behavior didn't make it any easier to shake off, though. I was miserable, it was bound to shine through. However, it wasn't her fault, though admittedly, I sometimes forgot. She was my mom after all.

Well, this was my life again. I'd have to learn to live with it.

Chapter 2

The day I returned to school came sooner than expected. Harvey picked me up a little earlier than he would have normally, because he figured it would be good for me to escape the rush.

"Dude, what are you wearing?" He snorted when I climbed into his beat-up, second-hand Volvo.

I looked down on myself. Non-descript T-shirt, jeans, sneakers. It had been warm for the past week, so I hadn't even bothered with my letterman jacket. "Clothes."

Take away the gold chains around Harvey's neck and the baseball cap, and our outfits weren't that different once he removed his oversized hoodie.

Exasperated, he shook his head, but started to drive at least. I knew what he meant. Not that long ago I would've dressed differently. But now, after everything I'd gone through, simple just seemed easiest. I had no reason to try to stand out, to make my mark in *high school*, of all places. I wasn't looking for a girlfriend anymore, and I didn't really care if the kids at the top of the high school food chain approved of me. I knew what was important to me. The opinion of someone overly full of themself sure as hell wasn't it.

Mitchell's Creek, Pennsylvania. Not a big place by any standard, but at least we had a high school. Go us. School colors: purple and yellow. In other words, a complete and utter eye sore.

Walking up to the main building felt weird. Familiar on one hand, but also like the last time had been about a million years ago. It felt like I had outgrown this place. Truthfully, it did make me somewhat curious. What had changed? What was still the same? Rationally, I knew that changes would be minimal. I'd been out for four months, not four years, after all. And yet, the feeling remained.

I found my locker quickly, but I struggled to remember my combination. I'd never bothered to change it from the school's setting, because it had seemed like more of a hassle at the time, but now it left me staring at the lock with a frown.

"Seven-four-three-nine," Harvey said, and I set the lock. "Your folks had them open the lock in case there was something important in there."

I didn't see what Mom could possibly have expected to find in my locker, but hey, it worked out for the best, so I didn't overly mind. I still wouldn't bother changing the combination. It wasn't like I kept anything worth stealing in there, and I'd never been bullied.

Pushing aside my gym bag—yeah, that was going to be washed tonight—I grabbed my algebra and world history books, replacing them with the lunch Mom packed for me.

"You got Algebra first, too?" Harvey asked. "It's in the new building. Mrs. Hammond teaches it now."

I grimaced at the sound of it. I remembered that teacher well from last year. Mrs. Hammond was a very tall and friendly lady with good intentions in becoming a teacher but was completely and utterly unsuited for the profession. She couldn't deal with conflict, had a weak voice, was prone to crying, and honestly, wasn't all that good at math.

Well, classes awaited.

I moved to follow Harvey when a call made me stop and look around.

"Ben!"

A girl I'd seen in some of my classes last year (or four months ago) came running up to me. She was wearing a cheerleader's uniform, her blonde hair in pigtails with purple ribbons tied around them.

"I heard you'd be back to school today," she said and gave me a broad smile. Her blue eyes practically sparkled at me. "I'm so glad you're feeling better again."

While she was talking, I was still struggling to remember her name. I knew we'd spoken at some point, but I couldn't remember the particulars of that either. It had been a while. For me, at least.

"You know, a few of us were gonna go to the mall later, some guys, too. Would you like to come?"

"Sure," I said. "Mind if I bring Harvey?"

He'd never forgive me if I didn't.

She beamed at me and nodded vehemently before running—or jumping? It was really difficult to tell with cheerleaders—off to go to whatever school activity she had lined up now. I turned to look for Harvey, but apparently, he hadn't noticed me stopping, because he was gone. Cursing under my breath, I jogged to catch up to him on the way to the new building.

"She's cute, eh?" He grinned at me when I finally caught him.

"Who?"

"Vivi. Obviously."

I remembered now. Vivienne was her name. But I still drew a blank about when we'd met before. I just knew it had happened.

"Feel like hanging with her and her friends later?"

Harvey stopped mid stride. "Uhm. Hello? Cheerleaders?"

"What about them?" I knew what he was saying, but it was so dumb I was actually kind of enjoying playing stupid.

Sighing, he put a hand on my shoulder.

"Cheerleaders. Are. Hot," he spelled it out for me, smirking conspiratorially. "I like hot chicks. It's simple math, doofus."

Ah, yes. Math. His favorite subject. Harvey plus cheerleader equals goal.

"I'm guessing that's a yes then," I said, walking past him.

Now he was the one who jogged to catch up with me. "You know what that means, right?"

"Hm?"

"She's got the hots for you."

No sooner had he said that, than I was reconsidering whether I should really go after all. Before, it had just been a friendly hangout. Now it was a *thing*. And a *thing* was as good as cheating on Tara and that … just wasn't cool with me.

We lived in different worlds, and as far as anyone here was concerned, she was my "girlfriend who lived super far away and didn't have a phone and also I don't have pictures of her, but she's totally real, I swear." In other words, in this world, she didn't exist. Quite literally. But that didn't mean she didn't exist to me, as weird as that sounded.

Harvey read my silence correctly. "Dude, you're seriously thinking about your imaginary girlfriend *now*? This is a real-life woman … and she *likes* you."

I shrugged. I'd tried explaining it to Harvey before, and he didn't get it. I couldn't really blame him. If our roles were reversed, I wasn't sure I would either.

"I'll still go," I decided. "But it won't change anything about the facts."

He rolled his eyes. "The fact that you're insane, you mean."

Thankfully, our arrival at the classroom saved me from the rest of that conversation.

Since I'd started to see my shrink, I didn't deal well with being called crazy. Before that, I hadn't really minded, somehow, don't ask me why.

Vivienne and her friends waited for us in the mall's food court after school. Now this was a place I hadn't come to all that often before. I'd never liked the crowds and noise. I liked my open spaces, thankyouverymuch. Still, spotting them was easy. There wasn't much that stood out more than the hideousness of our school colors on their uniforms.

"Ben, over here," Vivienne called out.

Boy, she actually jumped up from her seat to wave. That was, until one of her friends whispered something to her, with a glance at us. Vivienne faltered and blushed, sitting back down with a smile at us. One more small gesture to beckon us over, and that was it. Harvey was already halfway there, snatching us two chairs along the way to drag them over.

Then, introductions were in order. Aside from Vivienne, there were two other girls and one guy who had his arm around one of the girls. I recognized him. Pretty sure he was on the football team. Rod, his name was. Short for Rodney. His girlfriend, Lauren, was in my English Lit class. The last girl I didn't recognize. She introduced herself as Cindy, and based on her uniform, was a cheerleader like the other two.

True to form, Harvey immediately tried to monopolize her attention, nudging me toward Vivienne with his elbow.

"I'm gonna get a soda," I announced. "You want one, Harv?"

"Coke," he grumbled, before turning his attention back to the girl.

"I'll come with." Vivienne hurriedly followed me.

I walked slowly to allow her to catch up with me.

"I wasn't sure if you'd really come." She giggled nervously.

I glanced at her. "Why wouldn't I?"

"Well," she was looking everywhere except me as she fumbled for the words, "I guess you just don't seem the type to just hang out in places like this."

"I'm not," I agreed. "But after you invited me, I felt I kinda had to."

Whoops. Judging by the guilty look on her face that was the wrong thing to say. *Crap.*

"It's a nice change of pace," I added quickly. "It's good to change things up every once in a while."

Her face lit up. "I totally agree!"

It was now our turn in the queue. I ordered two sodas, and she ordered a burger.

I was surprised. I had to admit I was still under the impression that cheerleaders mainly ate salads or air, like in the movies. Although, clearly, I'd never interacted much with any real ones.

"You know," she said, slowing her pace, "I was really worried about you when you were … you know. The whole school was pretty shocked."

Not surprising. It was probably the most exciting thing that happened in this place in about a year.

"Did you get my card?" she asked. "I brought it to the hospital with Cindy, in like December, or something."

Truthfully, I'd received plenty of cards, but I hadn't looked at any of them. While it was nice that people thought of me, I knew it wouldn't make me happy the way I'd felt since coming back.

"Yeah," I lied. "Thank you for that."

She smiled brightly and then skipped ahead to rejoin our table. Honestly, it didn't really make a difference if I was there or not. Harvey was invested in talking to Cindy, and Rod and Lauren only spoke to each other, with an occasional inclusion of Vivienne.

I soon found myself staring off into space, listening intently to the noise around me and separating the different sources, analyzing them. None of the sounds seemed threatening or out of place. There was nothing to worry about. Not here. Not on Earth. Not in Mitchell's Creek.

Suddenly, I realized that I'd been asked a question. "What?"

Vivienne smiled at me. "I was just asking if you'd like to come."

Come to what?

"Um … Sure."

Harvey had probably been listening. I'd figure it out later. And I could always change my mind.

"Great! Then we should exchange numbers, so I can text you, 'kay?" She seemed oddly excited.

After no more than a few seconds, she was one of my twenty contacts. I wished Tara was in there, too. Maybe I should set up a fake number for her, just so her name was in my phone. I could even commission an artist to create a portrait of her that I could set as my background picture. It was stupid, but it'd probably make me feel better. At least create the illusion that I could talk to her whenever I wanted.

As if on cue, my phone rang. Mom.

"Sorry, gotta take this," I said, and left the table to find a quieter spot to talk to her. "Hey, Mom."

I was greeted with an audible sigh of relief. A pang of guilt shot through me. I hadn't even thought of letting her know I'd be meeting people before coming home.

"Ben, honey," her voice sounded forcefully chipper. "I just called to ask when you'd be home for dinner."

Liar.

"I'm safe, Mom," I said. "I just went to the mall with some friends. But I'll come home now. See you soon, 'kay?"

"Do you need a lift?" she asked, almost hopefully.

"That'd be great. I'll wait on the western parking lot. Thanks, Mom. You're the best."

"See you soon."

We hung up, and I stared at my phone for a moment.

I sometimes forgot how hard it had been on my mom, with my dad being away all the time, and her son in a coma. Probably still was, too. For a little while at least, I could probably play into her overprotectiveness, to help her feel more at ease again. After all, it wasn't like I was going to get hit by a truck again.

I glanced back at the group, who still chatting away, though Vivienne kept glancing back at me.

I decided to text her instead of going over.

My mom. Gotta go—she's worried.

I waited 'til she received the message and read

it, then gave a little wave and left.

Harvey wouldn't care that much about me leaving without him. He was keeping busy enough talking to Cindy.

I decided to wait by the mall's west entrance. It would take Mom about ten minutes to get here, but I figured I would enjoy the fresh air more than the cramped, overcrowded space in the food court.

I was watching the clouds pass slowly in the sky, when I saw a sudden movement of a large, dark shape out of the corner of my eye.

A Corrupted One!

All of my fighting instincts kicked in immediately, and I fell into a defensive stance, my senses on high alert. I was ready to strike.

Ready to strike a flag that had changed direction when the wind changed. My little stunt had gained me a few odd looks and giggles from some younger girls, but I didn't pay them any mind. Dropping my hands, I buried them in my pockets, to make sure they'd stay there.

I was back home now. These instincts I'd developed … they had to go. In this world, there was no place for them. No need for them. And chances of my ever returning to Halastaesia were sadly next to nonexistent. I needed to get used to this again. Allow this to become my new old normal.

CHAPTER 3

"I thought I saw one of them yesterday," I told Dr. Steinberg toward the end of our session. "And all of my old habits kicked in immediately, without thinking about it. It's like, for just a second, I was back to Halastaesia, ready to fight."

"And what happened when you realized you were still here and there were no evil monsters to battle?"

"I felt … a little silly. And I realized I have to really accept that I'm here now, or I'll just keep making everyone worry."

I felt defeated saying that. There was no way for me to return, and I had to accept that. Tara, Ronan, Phillip—they were people of the past now. Though, I wasn't quite ready to give up on them yet. Not entirely, anyway. Definitely not Tara.

I looked at Dr. Steinberg, who was smiling.

"That's a fantastic step forward," she said. "To embrace your here and now will greatly improve your life."

I gave a non-committal grumble in response.

"Why do you think you saw one of the monsters?" she then asked, her eyes narrowing ever so slightly.

I shrugged. "I've been so used to expecting them to show up out of nowhere, anywhere, anytime. I always find myself looking for dangers, listening out for weird sounds, odd movements, that kind of stuff."

"Hm." Staring at her notepad, Dr. Steinberg kept her face passive except for a slight twitch in her nostrils while she read over some of what she had written. Then she raised her gaze to meet mine. "Let's go back to your accident for a moment. Tell me about what you saw and felt when it happened."

I closed my eyes to allow my memories to settle. It had been over a year for me, but the moment was ingrained in my memory as if it had been only a week ago.

"I was cycling, going down the hill where I needed to take a left to go to school," I said quietly. "I tried to brake for the turn, but it wouldn't work. The ice just made me slide off. And then, out of nowhere, there was the truck."

I grew silent. Wearing headphones at the time, I hadn't been able to hear it coming, but I hadn't been paying much attention to my surroundings anyway. Not even a truck barreling my way had made it into my conscious mind. By the time I'd seen it, it had already been too late.

"I see." She sat up in her chair. "I'd like to give

you something to think about at home."

Curious about what she was going to suggest, I sat up as well.

"I'd like you to think about whether you can see any similarities between the truck, and the monsters you fought. And keep up that dream journal. Looking at your nightmares from a more objective point of view when you're awake should help you as well."

I got up. "Thanks, Doc."

She smiled. "Take care."

I left her office and headed to the parking lot where Mom waited in the car. Biking home from here wouldn't have taken more than ten minutes, but Mom preferred to drive me. After everything that had happened, I couldn't blame her.

"How was it?" she asked when I got in.

Grimacing, I shrugged. "She gave me home-work."

"Like the journal?"

"Kinda."

She put the car in gear and smiled. "I had a dream journal once."

"Oh yeah?"

"It didn't last for long." She put her blinker on to enter the road. "I could never really remember my dreams all that well."

Yeah, I didn't have that problem. My nightmares were vivid. Lifelike enough to almost make me believe I was back in

Halastaesia.

Almost.

"Dad's going to be home this weekend," she then said. "He just called."

"Awesome." I meant it. Having him back here was rare enough, and it'd be good for Mom, too. Maybe spending time together as a family would help them recover a little. There were still shadows under their eyes a lot, shadows that hadn't used to be there.

I glanced at Mom. Even now, despite the make-up she'd used to cover it up, the dark circles were clearly visible. I'd seen people with these circles back in Halastaesia. Tara also had them when I'd first met her. It was a mark of those who had lost everything that had been important to them.

There was a quiz in my Bio class the next day, but I was exempt from it since I'd missed everything that was going to be on it. So I just sat there, reading my world history textbook instead. Tara had been fascinated when I'd told her about my world. She'd always wanted to know more. I loved that thirst for knowledge. It was awe-inspiring.

Phillip, on the other hand, had been outraged by what I told him. Especially the part about my country rejecting the monarchy. Though neither of them could quite believe the tale of the Boston Tea Party. They'd called it a waste of resources.

Oh well. No matter what I learned from now on, I wouldn't ever have a chance to share it with them.

Gloomily, I looked over my class. Cindy was in it, sitting toward the back, scribbling furiously on the sheet of paper. I wondered if she'd ever given Harvey her number the other day. I hadn't gotten around to asking, and besides, I hadn't seen him much since then. Mom had driven me to school when it looked like he was going to be late.

At least I had something to look forward to this afternoon. I was going back to my MMA club, so I'd get to hang with Jack for a bit. Getting to spar with someone would feel good for a change. At least I wouldn't completely go out of shape. Well. Any more than I already had since December.

Thinking about sparring with Jack lifted my mood enough that by the time lunchtime came around, I was actually half decent company. I met up with Harvey on the way to the cafeteria, and no sooner had we gone through the door than I heard Vivienne's voice. "Ben, Harvey! Over here!"

She waved us over. Harvey sauntered to the seat next to Cindy and quietly said something to her that made her giggle. Okay, apparently that was something that was normal now. By some unspoken law or high school rule, we'd now become part of their clique. Even Rod gave me a friendly nod when I sat down.

It was everything I'd ever wanted. High school acknowledgement. Yay.

I could feel the gazes of other kids on us, people who knew us, or of us, and were wondering how and why this change had come about. Feeling them watch us gave me the creeps. Once again, I found myself listening out for any sound indicating a threat.

"You guys coming to the pep rally later?" Lauren asked.

"Obviously!"

I looked over at Harvey. He grinned widely at Lauren, clearly feeling in his element already. His hand was leaning on Cindy's chair, practicing for its future place around her shoulders.

"What about you, Ben?" Vivienne smiled sweetly.

I shook my head. "I've got training."

"You do sports?" Rod asked, his brows furrowed as though he were trying to remember which team I was on.

"Oh yeah, you do martial arts, don't you?" Vivienne's smile grew more brightly.

I glanced at her, surprised.

For a girl I didn't actually remember talking to before, she really knew a lot about me. "Yeah,

MMA."

Suddenly, Harvey's elbow was leaning on my shoulder. "My buddy here was ranked top ten in the regionals last year."

I rolled my eyes. Yes. I came tenth. Just about still warranted being placed I guessed. And regionals really weren't a big deal. Not in my weight class. Not in Pennsylvania. Nationals, on the other hand, that was interesting.

"That's really cool," Vivienne said.

A comment like that from a girl like her would have floored me a year ago. Now, it left me cold.

"Thanks." I gave her a thumbs-up. "Good luck at the pep rally. Knock 'em dead and all that."

She beamed at me and put her arms in a playful fighting stance. "We will!" She punched the air twice, with, admittedly not too bad form for someone who had no training.

"What the actual hell, dude?" Jack panted. "When did you get so fast?"

We'd been sparring for only ten minutes, but he was totally out of breath, sweat streaming down his face. I was out of breath, too, but I'd learned some tricks and better breathing techniques in Halastaesia that helped me recover quicker.

"I thought I was gonna have to go easy on you

since you were out so long. Man!"

He stemmed his hands on his knees, leaning forward. Pleased with my achievement, I grinned.

"I told you, I trained plenty."

He shot me a glance that was halfway stuck between admiration and annoyance. "Yeah, well, training in your dreams doesn't count or I'd be a freakin' superstar by now."

I chuckled quietly. Admittedly, I was a little surprised at how well my body responded to my mind, because Jack was half right—my body in this world *had* been stationary. I was definitely weaker than I'd been before, but what I'd lost in muscle mass I was able to make up for in things I'd learned that didn't rely on strength. And those movements had become instinctual, making me all the faster.

I couldn't wait to see how good I'd be once I was back in top form.

"Alright, let's go again. This time I won't hold back!" He dropped into his stance, and I followed suit. No holding back it was.

Instead of waiting for him to attack, I went first, faking out an attack from above, when I dropped low at the last moment and swept his feet. As soon as he hit the ground, I was on top of him, holding him in place until he tapped out.

He groaned. "I don't know how you learned this stuff, but you seriously gotta teach me."

"I guess I could share a secret or two with

you."

Having the upper hand on him felt good. Especially since he'd beaten me at the regionals, coming in at sixth place.

I helped him up.

"Hey, David's parents are out of town because it's a long weekend, and David and I are gonna have a little party at his place. Wanna come? Harvey already said he'd bring a girl." He rolled his eyes.

"Lemme check with my folks. They've been a little on edge since you-know-what. I might need to give them a little more time before I go back to full teenager on them."

He clapped my shoulders. "I hear ya, man."

Yeah, I figured he'd get it. Living alone with just his mom, he appreciated having a parent who actually cared.

"How's the therapy going, by the way? You started going, right?"

"It's fine." I didn't really know what else to say about it. He didn't want details, and I didn't want to provide them.

"Nice. Glad to hear it."

We wandered over to the bench to grab a drink.

"It's good to have you back, man. No one else can give me a challenge here." He surveyed the other sparing groups. "I was worried I might lose my touch without a worthy adversary." He playfully punched my shoulder.

"Well you got him back," I retorted. "And he's back with a vengeance."

Training like this felt good. It felt *real* good. Exercising my body this way, teaching it how to respond to threats, it was reassuring.

And even though it made all of my muscles feel like they were complete mush and my lungs burned like fire on steroids, I'd have happily gone for another few hours.

CHAPTER 4

I didn't end up going to Jack's party. Instead, I enjoyed a casual, intimate game night with my parents.

"Alright, champ, you and me, got it? We'll see who knows more about," Dad checked the box, "Norwegian artists." He dropped his stance and stood up, dropping his arm. "Nah, we can't do this." He turned to Mom. "Molly? I know you said obscure, but I didn't think you meant impossible. Do you have anything a little more … I don't know, American?"

I almost snorted. Leave it to Dad to know a lot about his own country but nothing at all about anywhere else in the world. Not that I knew more than one Norwegian artist either, if even that.

"How about American fighter jets?" I suggested with a cheeky grin.

I knew he wouldn't be able to resist it. After all, being in the army, this should be his turf. But my experience with strategy and empire building games alongside flight simulators should give me an edge as well. I considered it a fair fight.

"You're on." He narrowed his eyes and got back into his battle stance. It was what I'd call Gamer mode, but hey, to each their own.

Mom was at the computer, going through Wikipedia for random trivia about fighter planes to ask us. We both had squeaky toys we'd squeeze when we were certain we knew the right answer. If the first person got it wrong, the second got their shot before the answer was revealed.

It was a longstanding tradition in our house to play quizzes this way, when we didn't buy a set, like the Norwegian artists.

"Which was the first jet-engine fighter aircraft built in the USA?"

Mom was starting us off with an easy one. Both of our toys wheezed before she'd even finished the question, but mine had been just that little bit faster. Smirking at him, I gave him my answer.

"The Bell P-59 Airacomet."

Mom nodded. "And when?"

This time Dad was quicker. "World War II."

Question after question followed while Dad and I were getting more and more into it, racing each other for who could buzz first, triumphant smirks plastered across our faces when the other person got an answer wrong.

I was loving it. And so was Dad. His eyes were practically sparkling with fight. I doubted that they'd had many game nights while I'd been away. All the more reason to make up for lost time now.

"I'm getting hungry," I said. "Pizza anyone?"

"I could use a bite," Mom admitted.

Dad decided to take on the job of putting the frozen disks in the oven. "How are things going at school?" he called from the kitchen. "Everything going okay?"

"Yeah, catching up is easy enough."

"Anyone giving you any trouble?"

I chuckled to myself, and, sharing a glance with Mom, theatrically rolled my eyes. "No, Dad. I'm not getting bullied."

Coming back into the room, he grinned at me. "Never can be too careful. What about girls? Anyone catch your eye?"

"Howard," Mom warned, but he only shrugged.

"Or boys, I'm not fussy."

While it was nice that my parents were as open-minded as they were, they clearly hadn't caught up to the fact that I was still hung up on my girlfriend from another world. At this point, I didn't think that was going to change. It was easier to just pretend that I was leaving it all behind, pretend that it really was all just a dream, than to create conflict over something I could never prove to anyone. "No, Dad. I'm not exactly the most popular guy in school."

Vivienne popped into my head. Okay, well, maybe *one* girl liked me, for whatever reason. I still half suspected some ploy or bet behind her behavior.

"Hm," he said. "Weird."

Frowning, I raised one eyebrow in distrust. "Why?"

"Well," he said, putting my phone on the table, "because you got a text from a certain 'Vivi' asking if you wanted to go see a movie tomorrow."

Crap. I must have left my phone in the kitchen when I'd gotten a drink.

"Howard!" Mom's stern gaze did wonders.

"What?" He shrugged helplessly, albeit somewhat guiltily. "It's not like I *tried* to see it. It just popped up with that *driiing* sound."

She sighed, defeated, an accumulation of decades of repeated behaviors.

"It's fine, Mom," I said, smiling. He wasn't a super controlling father and certainly didn't have a history of reading my texts on purpose. But perhaps it was time that I set my phone to actually lock instead of always openly showing everything. I'd never bothered before, because it seemed like more effort to unlock it every time I got a message, which didn't happen all that often in the first place, but maybe my parents didn't need to have access to all my communications.

Picking up the phone, I scrolled through the message myself.

Hey, Ben, just wondering, do you still wanna come see *Starcrawl* in the cinema with us

tomorrow? It starts at 8pm. xoxoVivi

Starcrawl, huh? I'd seen trailers for that movie before my accident. Some form of sci-fi adventure. I couldn't quite recall the details, but I remembered being intrigued by it.

"You should go," Mom said, smiling softly.

Dad nodded his assent.

With them practically having made the choice for me, all that was left for me was to text back.

I'll be there.

Short and sweet.

No need to sign my name—she had me saved in her phone after all.

My parents shared a glance, one that I didn't like at all. I'd swear, I'd never met parents who were so eager to see their son dating. Just as long as they didn't start asking for grandkids before I was through college.

I'd been waiting in front of the cinema for about fifteen minutes when Vivienne arrived. I'd gotten there half an hour early, just in case, and I'd already scoped out the place, so I could position myself in a place where I could survey the area easily without leaving myself open to being snuck up on.

Vivienne was all dressed up in a mini-skirt, thigh-high socks, and a tank top. I was pretty sure she'd also done something with her hair, but I couldn't for the life of me figure out what it was.

"Have you been waiting long?" she asked with concern, jogging the last few steps, but I shook my head.

I glanced over her outfit again. "Aren't you going to freeze?"

They had ventilation in movie theaters because of the amount of people that came to the big movies. Stupidly, they never seemed to turn it down for less people which just meant that the room could be baltic. I usually didn't mind, but girls got cold so easily. And then they never dressed to prevent it. Such impractical thinking. Tara was always prepared for every eventuality.

"I'm sure I'll be fine. Besides, it's too late now, so let's go!"

I was about to ask if we weren't going to wait for the others, when I realized that there were no others. She'd tricked me into a date. If I'd ask, she'd probably say something like they'd all canceled for personal reasons. Turned out movies really *did* get it right.

Silently asking Tara for forgiveness, I sighed and followed Vivienne into the hall. We found our seats and I crossed my arms, for safety. I didn't want to risk having her try to hold my hand or anything, and I did still want to be able to enjoy the movie. Afterward, I'd need to tell her that I had a girlfriend. I didn't want to lead her on, after all.

While we waited for the movie to start, I kept a close eye on anyone entering the hall, taking mental notes on where everyone was seated. Luckily, Vivienne had chosen the seats at the very back—not ideal for the movie experience, but excellent for keeping an eye on my surroundings.

By the time the ads finished, the theater was barely half filled. It made sense; the film had already been out for several weeks, and it hadn't exactly broken the box office. Still, I expected it would be entertaining enough.

As the movie went on, I noticed Vivienne deliberately placing her hand on the seat division between us, clearly hoping I would take the next move and place my hand on top of hers. Well, fat chance.

Stoically ignoring her subtle attempt, I kept my arms crossed, and my eyes fixed on the screen in front of me. I couldn't fully let myself be absorbed into the movie though. Any time someone in the audience made a sound, or moved, alarm bells started ringing in my head. The ominous music from the film wasn't helping either.

"But how did this happen?" the movie's heroine said.

The screen flashed.

"But how did this happen?" the heroine repeated.

I frowned. That was the same scene as just before.

"How did this happen?"

It was shorter this time.

"This happen?"

"Happen?"

"Pen?"

"Pen?"

"Pen?"

It repeated over and over. Someone in the cinema laughed, while others groaned.

My eyes were fixed on the screen, my heart racing. All I could hear was the repetition of my name. Ben. Ben. Ben.

Then, the screen flashed again, and the movie continued, normally.

"They better give us our money back for that," someone said. His comment was met by laughter from his friends.

Noticing that my fingers were digging painfully into my arms, I released my grip slowly and took some deep breaths to calm myself. It was fine. There'd just been a mix up in the back. Despite my internal reassurances, adrenaline continued to rush throughout my body and my hairs were standing on edge, my nerves blank. All I wanted was to jump up and run out, but I forced myself to stay all the way to the end of the movie.

Vivienne giggled when we left the hall. "That has *never* happened to me before! Wasn't that so weird?"

Now was my chance to set the record straight. "Yeah, my girlfriend's never going to believe this."

I could almost hear her heart shatter. Her smile froze and her eyes widened. "Your girlfriend? I had no idea you were seeing someone. What's her name?"

She tried too hard to sound casual. I genuinely felt bad for her, but better now than later, right?

"Yeah, her name's Tara. She lives pretty far away, so we don't get to see each other a lot."

"Oh." She gulped and tried to force another smile. "Long distance must be rough, huh?"

"You have no idea."

I knew I sounded miserable. Unfortunately, that was my downfall.

A moment of awkward silence expanded between us before Vivienne, shifting her weight and clutching one elbow with her other hand, cleared her throat.

"I know it's not my place to say," she began, tentatively, "but shouldn't love be easy? I mean, whether you're close by or far apart, it shouldn't eat away at you, right?"

In a way, her advice wasn't that terrible. Which made it all the worse considering where it came from. It would have been much easier to accept and appreciate if she hadn't made her intentions so obvious.

Besides, loving Tara had never been hard.

Relationships needed to be worked at, obviously, but we'd always figured it out by talking openly and honestly. Well, until I was thrown back into my own world. That had kind of thrown a spanner in the works.

"It doesn't, really," I said. "I just wish I could see her more."

"I guess I can understand that. Have you guys been together for long?"

I nodded. Time had passed differently in Halastaesia. The three months that I'd been in a coma had been a lot longer there. "Almost a year."

I could see her brain trying to work something out, but I couldn't quite figure out what it was. Still, she gave me an odd look just before she glanced at her watch.

"I should go home," she said. "Thanks for coming tonight. I'll see you at school!"

She whisked off, leaving me alone in front of the cinema. I'd told Mom I'd text her when the movie was out, but I hesitated. Thoughts were still racing through my head, and I needed some time to sort them.

There'd been something in the look Vivienne had given me. A certain level of distrust, and many, many questions. Some pain, too. I bet she'd heard from Harvey that I was single, and now thought that I was lying about Tara just to ward her off. Which was half true, at least.

I couldn't get what had happened with the

movie out of my mind either. Ben. Ben. Ben. Of course it could have been a weird coincidence, but it felt too poignant to me to believe it. And there was a tiny glimmer of hope that by some strange magical means, someone from Halastaesia had tried to get into contact with me.

I just hoped it wasn't because something terrible had happened.

CHAPTER 5

I didn't tell Dr. Steinberg about what had happened at the cinema. After all, I went to her in order to get used to my life here again, not to tell her about potential messages from Halastaesia. She didn't need to help me with anything real, she only needed to help me with my phantoms. My PHD. My Post-Halastaesia-Disorder.

I did open up about the situation with Vivienne though, telling her about Tara.

"I felt bad about it," I said. "I didn't like her thinking I was lying to her just to get her off my back. She deserves better than that."

"Why not explain the situation to her?" Dr. Steinberg suggested.

I scoffed, throwing my hands up in exasperation. "So I go to her and say, 'Hey, by the way, that girlfriend I mentioned? I met her while I was in a coma in a different world.' Yeah, I'm sure that's going to help my situation."

Dr. Steinberg smiled in response. "Your feelings are what matter here. Whether Tara exists in this world or not, does not change that you are experiencing romantic feelings for her. If Vivienne is the sort of girl you describe her to be, don't you think she may be able to understand and respect that?"

I gave myself a moment to think about it. If anyone would accept my feelings on the matter, it would probably be Vivienne. But she might also see it as a chance to take Tara's place in my heart.

"Have you tried speaking to Tara at all since you've returned?" Dr. Steinberg asked suddenly.

I looked at her, befuddled. "Um. No? She lives in another world. I can't exactly just call her up and say hey, how you doin'?"

"You could write her a letter."

A letter. Honestly, it had never occurred to me. I could write down everything I wanted to say to her, and then burn it or something, and hope that by some magical miracle or other, it would reach her.

"I might just do that."

She smiled again. "Wonderful. Then, I'd like to return to the assignment I gave you last time. Have you thought about it?"

She was talking about the question whether I saw any similarities between the truck that had hit me and the monsters I'd fought in Halastaesia. I shook my head.

"Not really. A lot has been going on. I've been keeping up my dream journal though."

I sat up to pull it out of my bag, but Dr.

Steinberg shook her head and reached out with a hand to stop me. "I don't need to see it. The journal is just for you, to face your dreams with a rational mind and have a chance to think on them."

That seemed a little pointless.

"So let's think about the similarities now, shall we?"

Sighing, I laid back down and closed my eyes to think better. "I guess both came out of nowhere and can be instantly lethal?"

That was all I could come up with on the spot.

"Why do you think they have that in common?"

Once again, I found myself looking up at her in bafflement. What kind of holistic reasoning was she looking for? That was like asking why both chairs and stars existed.

Unless … Unless she was asking me with the assumption that we were in agreement that the Corrupted Ones were figments of my imagination. In which case, the answer she was looking for was a simple, obvious one.

"Because I projected everything I felt about the truck onto the monsters, maybe?"

She scribbled on her notepad but didn't share any sign of acknowledgement of what I said. "What about your role as hero slaying those monsters?"

I just stared at her. At some point she'd switched from talking to me while keeping whether Halastaesia was real or not out of the conversation, to assuming that we were in agreement that it wasn't. That it really was all just a coma dream. I'd almost missed the transition, too.

Apparently, she mistook my angry silence for confusion because she posed me a different question. "How did you feel in high school before your accident?"

She really had a knack for weird questions. I wondered if they were meant to lower my guard. This one was easy enough to answer though.

"Invisible."

About half of the school probably felt unseen and unheard. I certainly was no exception there. I'd had friends, sure, but not many. I'd been neither popular, nor bullied. I'd just ... floated, almost like a ghost.

The pen moved quickly as she wrote it down. "How did you feel in Halastaesia?"

On this I reflected for a moment. "Needed."

I was starting to see what she was getting at. "How about now?"

What did I feel? Not useless. Not invisible, either, though I actually wouldn't mind that too much. Certainly not needed. But also not *not* needed, either.

"Guilty," I settled.

"Guilty?" Dr. Steinberg set her notepad down, the slightest twitch in her eyebrows suggesting the hint of a frown. "Why is that?"

There were so many reasons that I could barely begin to put them all into words. "For having put my parents through such immense pain. For hurting Vivienne's feelings. For betraying Tara. For breaking the promises I made to my friends in Halastaesia. For not being completely honest with Jack and Harvey. For constantly lying to everyone. For not being able to choose either world. For letting everyone down."

The words fell from my lips, poured from them like a dam had been broken and the feelings could no longer be contained as its edges crumpled under the force. My throat closing up, I stared at the ceiling, allowing myself to admit what I'd lied to even myself about. The guilt was almost making me want to puke.

"For sometimes wishing I could just forget."

I didn't see Vivienne for two days after the incident at the movies.

That didn't stop Harvey from chewing me out.

"What the hell are you doing, man?"

Yep, that's how he greeted me Tuesday morning when he picked me up at my house.

"I *was* going to go to school, but now I'm thinking I should reconsider." I climbed into the car.

"No. I mean with Vivi."

"Vivi?" I raised an eyebrow. They were on nickname terms now?

"She told Cindy what happened, and Cindy told me."

Ah, yes. High school. I'd forgotten. Secrets and privacy basically didn't exist without at least half the school knowing about it already.

"You blew her off because of your *imaginary* girlfriend? I mean, seriously? It doesn't matter how hot the chick in your dream was, dude, Vivi is a real-life, flesh and blood woman. And she wants you. So why the hell are you going out of your way to blow this?"

I stayed silent. There was no way I could get him to understand. But I could feel the warmth from the ring around my neck. The ring that had come with me from Halastaesia. The ring connecting me to Tara.

I thought of the advice Dr. Steinberg had given me. That my feelings were valid in and of themselves, regardless of whether or not Tara was real. While Vivienne might understand that reasoning, Harvey definitely wouldn't.

"Look, can we not? You've got it cushy with Cindy, right? I just …" I fumbled, trying to find something that would get him to lay off me. "I just need some time, okay?"

He shrugged dismissively, focusing his attention on the road instead.

"For what it's worth, I think you're being a

dumbass, but it's your life, so ... whatever."

"Yeah, maybe."

The rest of the drive passed without any further conversation, and once we reached school, Harvey charged ahead, leaving me behind with ease. *Okay, so he's mad.*

Really, I thought that I should be the one who was angry, for having decisions imposed on me and basically being told I should just forget about my girlfriend and get with another girl because she was right in front of me, but hey, life was weird.

I headed to my Spanish class, but the teacher was out sick, so the sub told us to do whatever we wanted as long as we were quiet.

This was as good a time as any to write my letter to Tara. Except ... I couldn't. I didn't know what to say to her right now. Didn't know how to start. So I decided to write to Ronan instead.

Hey, bud, Ben here.

So remember how the silver-banded mages thanked me for my services, gave me a bunch of medals and all of that, and then said I had to go home? And then cast that spell?

Yeah. So, I'm back home. In my old world. Turns out that my body here was in a coma this entire time after an accident. And everyone is telling me that you guys and everything we've been through together was only a dream. What a joke, right?

But hold on, I haven't even told you the best part yet—they want me to forget, and pretend that nothing ever happened.

I feel at a loss here. I could really use a hand. Or a response of any kind. Y'know, whatever works.

Could you, like, smash down the barriers between our worlds with your crazy strength or something? That'd be really helpful.

Yeah. I didn't really think so either.

I know I didn't have a choice but … I'm sorry, dude, for disappearing like I did.

I don't think I'll be back, so you ride that dragon without me.

Look after Tara for me, 'kay? And my horse, too. And tell Old Garthon that he can keep the sword I left with him. Also, for Phillip—I came back and no, we STILL don't have the monarchy back. I guess you lost that bet.

Knowing that I can't come back … Well, I think I'm going to have to move on. Stop thinking about all of you with every breath I take. Focus on the people in front of me instead of the ones out of my reach.

I hope things are well on your side and that reconstruction is going smoothly.

Farewell.

Ben.

The clock rang out, but I didn't move.

I'd just poured out my heart on the paper, and it was a final goodbye. But saying goodbye didn't mean I was going to forget. It just meant that I couldn't keep looking back and let the past stop me from moving forward.

I ran into Vivienne in the hallway the next day. As in, we literally ran into each other when we tried to turn the corner like in some cartoon. The impact made the books she was carrying scatter across the floor.

"Dang, I'm sorry." I quickly knelt down to help her gather her stuff.

"No worries," she said quietly, and got down as well.

Leaning over, Tara's ring slipped out of my shirt, and I heard Vivienne give a small gasp. I looked up to find her staring at me, bewildered.

"You're wearing it," she finally said.

"What?"

"The ring." She pointed. "I left it for you at the hospital one of the times I visited, but I thought for sure it had gotten lost." She stood back up, and I followed. "But you're actually wearing it." The tiniest incredulous smile tugged at the corners of her lips.

My mouth suddenly went dry and my whole body was stiff and sluggish. "Oh," I said. "Yeah."

My brain was hurting.

This wasn't Tara's ring. Vivienne had left it for me at the hospital. She'd never been to Halastaesia, so she couldn't have gotten her hands on Tara's ring.

Of course. It didn't make sense that I could've brought it from Halastaesia myself. Even though it looked so much like Tara's ring, down to the encryption in fae.

Could there be two identical rings with the same message in two different worlds?

I was beginning to feel dizzy.

No. And that meant …

That meant …

I turned to ice.

"Hey, are you okay? Ben?" Vivienne peered into my face. "You don't look so well. Let me take you to the nurse."

I allowed myself to be pulled along behind her. Let her tightly grasp my hand.

The ring I'd held onto this entire time, the one and only thing that proved that my experience had been real, had nothing at all to do with it. It had been a gift from a girl who'd been crushing on a comatose high schooler.

And that meant …

Vivienne left me in the nurse's office. He checked my vitals and then told me to lay down for an hour. If I wasn't feeling better then, he'd call my parents to pick me up. Vivienne promised to come back and check on me after the class was over.

I barely responded to anything anymore. I wasn't even sure if I was really hearing them.

Everything Dr. Steinberg and I had spoken about flashed through my mind again.

I'd felt invisible before, so I'd become a hero.

The threat of the truck had been so unexpected and deadly, that I fought and bested monsters who resembled those aspects.

Girls had never looked at me twice, but suddenly I had a girlfriend who was ethereally gorgeous.

Because if Vivienne was the one who'd brought me that ring, that meant that Halastaesia and everyone in it really had been nothing more than a dream. A hyper realistic dream designed by my comatose brain to let my mind escape to cope with what happened to me, like the doctors said.

And that meant that even awake I'd still been half-stuck in that dream, causing those who cared about me in this world to suffer.

I was the worst.

Chapter 6

At home, I shut myself in my room. They'd called Mom to pick me up before school was out, but she'd had to go back to work because of an upcoming surgery on a Pomeranian, so I was alone at home, which suited me just fine. I didn't want to talk to anyone.

There were so many things I needed to sort out.

Trying to form coherent thoughts was futile; my brain was so overwhelmed, it flashed nothing but warning signs to the rest of my body, forcing adrenaline through my veins. Depressed as I already was, the added agitation only served to further frustrate me.

So instead of dealing with it, I turned to gaming for distraction.

The rest of the day was spent playing strategy games, mostly empire building and war games, to distract myself. I had a decent array of RPGs as well, but I didn't have the right mindset for them right now.

It was really no surprise my comatose brain had thought up a scenario like the fight against the Corrupted Ones. It was a straight-forward enemy that needed to be vanquished. There was no moral ambiguity. Forces needed to be assembled, and then a battle plan had to be drawn up. All of that was right up in my alley, thanks to these games.

Then, hand-to-hand combat. It was true that my fighting had gotten smarter in real life, but I could possibly attribute that to the fact that my brain had been working in my coma, trying to figure out better ways I could protect myself. It must have replayed things I'd seen on TV or at competitions, and "taught" them to me via the imaginary training in my dream.

Then it had conjured up friends to stop me from feeling lonely. A girlfriend because I'd never had one. It made me a hero because I didn't want to be invisible anymore, and it let me fight and defeat monsters to make up for the fact that I hadn't been able to protect myself in real life. A part of me must have also been aware of my real surroundings in the hospital since it had incorporated some things into my dream, like the ring Vivienne had given me. I imagined that I'd also overheard conversations that were somehow made part of the world I was dreaming up.

The more I thought about it, the more forcefully I tapped the buttons on my mouse and keyboard. Angrily, desperately.

I hated how neatly all of this was fitting

together.

And what I hated even more was that I hadn't realized it sooner.

Me? A hero? Yeah, right.

All I'd done was make other people worry about me, and still continued to do. Some hero I was.

I made a mistake in my game that cost me the lives of half of my fictitious people and flipped the keyboard in anger.

Enough of that.

After rushing down to the basement, I let out my frustration on my drum set instead.

I didn't even bother to wear mufflers.

The sounds of the drums, the vibrations that extended into my entire body—I reveled in it, lost myself in a frenzy of the cacophony of my creation. Only when my arms were aching and my ears were ringing painfully did I pause to take a few deep breaths.

I was feeling a little better. Not great by any means, but better. A tiny bit, anyhow.

And I realized that more than ever, I needed to talk to someone about my thoughts and this revelation. And I knew just the person.

"I have to admit, I was a little surprised to get your call," Dr. Steinberg said, frowning ever so slightly underneath her horn-rimmed glasses.

I'd been lucky—she'd had a cancellation in the afternoon and had agreed to see me on short notice. Since Mom hadn't even been home yet, and I couldn't find my bike, I'd taken the bus to get here.

"It's important," I repeated for the umpteenth time, to myself, and to her.

She nodded. "You said, yes."

She gestured toward the couch, and I didn't hesitate. Before she'd even taken her own seat, I was already talking. "It wasn't real. None of it was. It's exactly like everyone said—it was a dream induced by my comatose brain to deal with what happened to me. The trauma." I clenched my fists, angry at myself.

"What makes you say that?" she asked, though I thought I could detect a note of excitement in her voice. Encouragement.

"Well, it's true, isn't it? None of it was real. Everybody kept telling me, and I ..." I shook my head in disbelief at my stupidity. "I just kept sticking to it, convinced I knew better."

"What changed?"

Closing my eyes, I took a moment to formulate my scrambled thoughts into something coherent. "There was a ring," I said quietly, almost under my breath. "And that ring was given to me in my dream. But when I woke up, it was in my hand, and no one seemed to know where it had come from." I forced my breathing to remain steady, to breathe deeply, and slowly. "But I found out who gave it to me for real. And that kind of put everything in perspective. Everything you've made me think about as well. It all just suddenly fell into place and it's like … It's like I was looking at a picture of a night sky and I was convinced it was the real deal, and everyone kept telling me that it was just an imitation, just a picture, but I wouldn't believe them because I recognized one of the constellations. And then, someone made me put it down for just a moment and I finally saw the real sky." I shook my head. "It's just … It's so confusing."

Dr. Steinberg scribbled some stuff as I spoke. Her voice was gentle, comforting, and empathetic when she asked, "And how are you feeling now?"

"Confused." I chuckled miserably. "Angry. Regretful. Sad? I don't know."

"What is it you're regretting?"

I ground my teeth. God, what *wasn't* I regretting? I could barely even find a start. "Getting in that stupid accident in the first place," I said. "Turning Vivienne down. Being such an ass overall. Putting my parents and my friends through all of this, even now." I gave a mirthless laugh. "I've basically lost months I could've been spending with everyone, making up for lost time, by moping and whining about how I missed the people from my dream. How shitty is that?"

Gall was rising up in my throat when I thought about it. I seriously was the worst.

"Even now I'm still feeling sad that I can't see them again. They're not even real!" Noticing with some embarrassment that I had shouted the last part, I ran my hands through my hair, and then left them covering my eyes, frustrated.

Silence followed my outburst. Only the ticking of the clock in the corner and my heavy breathing disturbed the quiet. It felt so rapid, every tick chasing the one before, while also seeming like an eternity separated each one.

Dr. Steinberg set her notepad down on her little table before she spoke, calmly. "They were real to you. Your feelings for them were certainly real. The mind is a powerful thing. And it's not always reliable." She paused, to let her words sink in. "None of this is your fault."

Her words were comforting, if nothing else.

I sighed deeply.

"It's going to take time," she added. "You've gone through severe physical and mental trauma. Don't expect everything to go back to normal right away. Allow yourself the time you need to heal … in whatever capacity you need."

I could just about nod. What she said sounded right. It was advice I'd give Jack or Harvey if our roles were reversed.

"For now, you should continue to live normally the best you can. Surround yourself with people who care about you. Then, day by day, things will get easier."

I'd been right. Talking to her had been the right call. After my little outburst and her words, I felt much calmer. Almost at peace, even. I felt like I could finally, truly move forward.

Mom was in a frenzy when I got home. She came storming out into the hallway as I opened the door, her hair messy, her hands shaking as she pressed a phone to her ear.

When she saw me, tears welled up in her wide eyes and her lips quivered. "It's alright now, Officer, thank you. ... Yes, he just came in the door. I'm so sorry. Thank you. ... Yes, you have a nice evening as well."

She almost dropped the phone when she swooped toward me to pull me into a tight hug.

I'd done it again.

I hugged her back, stroking her back gently, until it finally stopped trembling. "I'm sorry, Mom," I said quietly. "I needed to go see Dr. Steinberg."

She pulled away from me to hold me at arm's length, tears having smeared her makeup. "Dr. Steinberg?" she asked, fear creeping into her voice. "Are you alright? You didn't ..."

I smiled warmly at her, trying to put her at

ease, and shook my head. "No, I didn't think of killing myself, don't worry." I led her to the living room and sat her down on the couch, before sitting next to her. "There was some important stuff that came up, is all, and it couldn't wait until Friday. But you know? I think things are finally going to be okay again."

I smiled at her, actually feeling calm, the fight within me about constant discontentment over. I'd finally woken up for real. I was home.

PART II

CHAPTER 7

I started cycling to school again. As it turned out, my parents had hidden my bike because Mom was nervous about letting me ride after the accident. But now that I was finally ready to turn over a new leaf, I'd managed to convince her that real normalcy was the best thing for me, and since riding my bike to school was normal for me she relented, albeit reluctantly.

Three weeks had passed since my grand revelation, but I continued to see Dr. Steinberg, though only once a week instead of the two to three times I'd done before. There was still some trauma I had to work through. A lot of it, actually.

After we bumped into each other in the hallway that day, Vivienne went back to interacting with me without awkwardness, much like she had done before our unfortunate movie date, though she was holding back a little. I was glad for it. While I wasn't exactly ready to jump into a real relationship right away, I did think I'd like it if it was with someone like her. She was a nice girl, smart and funny. And exceptionally cute. Now that I didn't have my fictional girlfriend constantly on the brain, I could actually appreciate that.

"Ben!" She waved at me when I arrived at school and came jogging over as I locked my bike.

"Hey, Vivi," I said. "What's up?"

"Guess what?" Her eyes were practically sparkling.

"What?"

"No," she pouted, "you have to guess!"

Alright, I'll play. "You won a car in the lottery."

She shook her head, sending her pigtails flying. Her grin only grew wider with each failed guess.

"You've been asked to model for a magazine."

She shook her head again and blushed ever so slightly.

"Your long-lost twin who lives in Mongolia just contacted you, telling you that you inherited a palace there and we're all invited to a huge party where we get to ride elephants?"

This suggestion elicited a laugh from her. And what a nice laugh it was. Clear and high, but not the annoying giggle I'd always associated with cheerleaders.

"Alright, I give up ... tell me."

She held a flyer she must have kept hidden behind her back before up to my face.

I skimmed it quickly. "A carnival?"

"Yes!" She was almost bouncing on the spot. "And they'll have a fireworks show on the opening night! Come on, we *have* to go, right? I haven't had a chance to talk to the others yet, but I'm sure they'll love the idea."

It was set for next month, and honestly, it looked like it would be a blast.

"Yeah, let's go, I'm up for that." I grinned at her.

She glanced at her watch. "Oh dang it, I forgot I have practice before class. See you at lunch!"

"Later."

And with that she was off, running toward the gym as if the devil was after her. For a moment, I watched after her with a bemused grin. That girl. I didn't think I'd ever seen her not wearing her cheerleader's uniform in school. And she always seemed to be in a hurry to either get to practice or was coming from practice to go to her classes — the exception being lunch time, of course.

"Hey, space cadet." Harvey waved a hand in front of my face. "What are you spacing out for?"

"No reason. Mornin'."

"Yeah, good morning to you, too." He grinned mischievously after glancing behind his back, lest a teacher should overhear. "So, mind if I copy your geography homework?"

I rolled my eyes and threw him my notes. "Just get it back to me before third period."

He saluted. "Aye, aye, capt'n!"

While the others hung out in the mall after school was out, I cycled over to the MMA club. Jack was already there, warming up.

"Ready to get familiar with the ground?" he asked, grinning.

"I sure hope you are!" I countered, with a smirk of my own.

I went through my own warm up routine before the training started. Our coach arrived just as I finished, and he put us through the usual drills before we were finally allowed to try out our new, improved techniques in sparring.

The last few weeks, Jack and I had trained with other partners to change it up, so we were both raring to have another go at each other. Me to see if I could still beat him or if last time had been a fluke, him to seek retribution and assert himself as the better fighter.

But whatever mojo my brain had cooked up while I'd been in a coma was still working, and I evaded and countered his attacks easily, while getting mine in without much difficulty. I was feeling better about this time, compared to our previous fight. My extra training had paid off—I was already stronger than I had been.

When we finally took a break to grab a drink,

Jack clapped my shoulder. "I think you might actually have a shot at the regionals this year."

I shrugged. I'd had the same thought, but I didn't want to jinx it. If I'd improved, so could the other fighters. "You're not so shabby either."

He chuckled. "Yeah, well, I gotta put in some work to catch up to you again."

Watching me as I rubbed the sweat from my face with my towel, he suddenly turned serious. "You seem like you've been doing better lately."

"You think so?"

"Oh yeah. Better than before the accident, even. You seem, like, more together if you know what I mean?"

I could kind of see where he was coming from. I was definitely more confident now. Happier with my situation in life, too. Almost losing everything had given me a new appreciation for what I had, and I felt like a better me.

I grinned at him. "Are you going mushy on me?"

"What? No way." He slapped his towel at me, but I got him right back.

"So," he said then, "you're still on for this weekend, right?"

"You better believe it."

Saturday at eleven a.m., Harvey picked me up

with his car, Jack already sitting in the passenger seat. Just before we turned into the car park of our destination, Jack turned back to me. "So, Harv and I have made a decision."

I raised an eyebrow. This was gonna be good. Harvey chuckled, and a mischievous grin broadened on Jack's face. "We're gonna turn this thing into a little competition."

I leaned forward. "I'm listening."

"You're gonna get wrecked," Harvey jeered jovially and parked the car. He turned around in his seat as well, a familiar glint in his eye. "Let's talk stakes."

"Whoever wins, gets to decide something for the other two."

Frowning, I scratched my head. "Isn't that a little broad?"

"Not if we set out the agreed terms right now," Jack said. "And we've already decided what you'll have to do if either one of us wins."

Ah. I'd been set up. And I had a strange feeling I could guess what their thing was about. "And what is that?"

Harvey grinned, evilly. "During spring break, we're all gonna do an escape room together. I'm gonna bring Cindy, and Jack's gonna bring David."

He didn't have to say it. I knew where this was going.

"And I'll have to bring Vivi," I stated.

They both grinned. Way to go, trying to force

me into a date. A group date, at that. Then again, what harm could come of it? Besides, if I won, *I* could get *them* to do something.

"Then if I win—" I said.

"Which you won't," Jack interjected, and we both grinned.

"We shall see. Then if I win, Harvey has to *actually* do his own homework for the rest of the year, and Jack, you have to dye your hair in a freaky new color."

Since their thing for me was meant to be for my own good, I figured I should return the favor.

We shook on it and headed into the GoKart lobby.

Fifteen minutes later, all geared up and safety-briefed, we took our seats in the Karts, raring to go. I was going to let them breathe my dust.

As soon as the light hit green, I set off. As did they. I'd started in the spot behind them, so I was weaving from side to side, trying to find any kind of opening to pass them. But they knew what they were doing. Whenever I tried to push past, they would drive in my way, snaking from side to side to give me no chance. To add to my frustration, I wanted to go ... no, *needed* to go fast and really feel the thrill of the chase, but any time I was able to pick up any speed, Harvey kept me in check by forcing me to brake. Meanwhile, Jack was already coming up behind me again.

I gritted my teeth. No way was I going to lose

to them!

Finally, I got my chance. Harvey took a corner too wide, leaving a gap, and I shot through, racing around the track like there was no tomorrow. Feeling the wind rush past the few gaps the gear left felt good, real good, and a grin had formed on my face before I knew it. This rush of speed, that's just what I needed. In no time at all, I'd come up behind Jack. Harvey crashed into a wall ahead of him, and raised his hand to request help from the staff. Jack and I used the opportunity to race like we were always meant to.

Down to the last minute, he stayed ahead of me, always managing to secure all angles, to cut me off at any possible moment so I could never get ahead of him. Jack wasn't afraid of speed, oh no, he lived on it, just as much as I did. But then, in the last few seconds, I still managed to push past him, taking the corner at a far higher velocity than was strictly safe.

I had this in the bag.

The lights changed and we all returned to the box. I met the others in the lobby, grinning as I took my helmet off.

"Guess you won this time," Harvey said, shaking my hand, smirking.

Jack couldn't hold back his laughter. "You can't say that as if you were anywhere close to beating him!"

"Yeah, well, you weren't that much better,

either."

"Wanna bet?"

We collected the records of our lap times and compared. All in all, both Jack and I had completed forty-three rounds, while Harvey managed a measly twenty-eight. I hadn't quite realized how often we'd lapped him.

"How are you so slow?" I asked in disbelief.

"Ever heard the story of the hare and the tortoise?"

I'd never seen him so sullen.

Meanwhile, there'd only been a few seconds between Jack and I, and my fastest lap had been eleven point three seconds, while his had been eleven point one.

Considering that his fastest speed had been better than mine …

"You still get your win," I decided.

They both looked up from their records.

"I'll take Vivi to the escape room over break. But you guys still have to do your things, too!"

Harvey groaned, but he grinned. "Works for me. I guess I've gotta go home and actually do some homework then."

Jack touched a strand of his dark brown hair and pulled it down so he could look at it. "And I guess I've got to decide on a new color."

Chapter 8

I could have texted Vivienne, but I decided I'd rather invite her to our outing in person. With that in mind, I headed to school early on Monday morning, knowing that she had cheer practice in the morning. I managed to catch her just as she finished.

"Hey, Vivi, can I talk to you for a moment?"

"Oh, hey, you're here early! Sure, what's up?"

She waved to Cindy and Lauren to head on without her, and they did, but not without whispering to each other, and several glances back to us.

Suddenly I could feel the heat of embarrassment creep up my neck and ears.

"Well, my friends and I are going to do an escape room over the break." My eyes kept darting around, never quite meeting hers. "And I was wondering if you'd like to come. I'm pretty sure Harvey is going to invite Cindy."

She lit up with excitement, and the brightest, happiest smile formed on her face. "Yes, absolutely! When is it?"

"Saturday, I think."

She nodded vehemently. "I'll be there! You can count on it."

"Awesome."

Ugh, why was I feeling so awkward? It hadn't been this difficult before. But suddenly I was hyper aware of her fruity scent and how long that skirt made her legs look and …

Calm down, Ben.

We walked up to the main building together, having switched conversation topics to school related stuff.

"You guys have been training a lot lately, do you have something coming up?"

Vivienne inclined her head casually. "We're preparing for the cheer-offs next month. But we also have another rally this week."

I glanced at her. She really enjoyed cheering, huh? She always had a little smile on her face when she talked about it, almost wistful, as if she wished she could be training right then and there. I remembered seeing the cheer squad before. They were good. And the amount of athleticism that went into it was no joke. I couldn't even dream of attempting half the stuff they made look as easy as a stroll in the park.

"When is it?" I asked. "I'd like to come."

Her gaze shot up to meet mine, and her eyes widened as her smile grew broader. "Really?"

I nodded.

Once again, she was practically bouncing on the spot. "It's on Thursday, after school out on the pitch. I can't wait!"

I felt like that should have been my line. "I look forward to it."

Her enthusiasm was contagious, and I found myself smiling alongside her. I was sure she'd be great. Someone who loved cheering that much and put as much work into it as she did just had to be great at it.

Even though it was early, the PA system suddenly turned on, but instead of principal O'Hara's voice, there was only crackling.

Vivienne and I looked at each other and burst out laughing.

"Think he accidentally put his coffee on the button?" I asked, grinning. "I bet in a second we're gonna hear him burp or something."

"Chosen One … Give it back to us …"

The whisper was barely audible over the crackling, but my blood suddenly froze, as did my grin.

No. It couldn't be true.

The announcement stopped after a few more seconds, and I laughed nervously.

"Did you hear that?" I grabbed the strap of my backpack. "The whispering?"

Vivienne frowned and then leaned forward, curious.

"No, I didn't. What did it say? Oh my god, does Mr O'Hara have a secret lover there?" She threw her hands to her face, covering her cheeks. "Is that why the PA system turned on? Were they ... doing it?"

Suffice to say she hadn't noticed a thing. I wasn't sure if that should be reassuring to me or not. I intensely hoped that it had been Harvey, playing a trick on me, because otherwise, I was hallucinating, and that couldn't bode well for me.

I asked Harvey the second he arrived at algebra class.

"The PA system?" he asked, frowning. "Dude, I was late. I played through my new game almost the entire night and passed out at some point." He shrugged and jovially clapped my shoulder. "You should try it. I think it's right up your alley."

I listened to him drone on about his new game, but my thoughts were elsewhere. I'd asked a few other people if they'd heard the whisper, but no one aside from me seemed to have heard anything except the crackling. That alone led me to the conclusion that I was going cuckoo. There was only one option ... I had to talk to Dr. Steinberg. All the better that I had an appointment with her after school today.

I didn't normally dislike school, but today of all days it seemed to drag on for ages. Eons, even.

But finally, the bell rang, letting us out, and I was on my bike and on my way to Dr. Steinberg's before most students had even left their classrooms yet. I knew I'd need to wait outside until our appointment, but at least I would already be around. Waiting there felt better than to take it easy and casually engage in the chatter that usually marked the end of a school day. And it meant that I could try to get my head straight in the time I spent waiting.

It didn't go as well as I'd hoped.

By the time my scheduled appointment came around, my thoughts were still whirling—a state I was beginning to become overly familiar with lately.

"You've been waiting for quite a while, Ben," Dr. Steinberg noted with amusement when I finally dropped into her couch.

"How did you …"

She pointed at the window. "I saw you pacing outside. So why don't we start by you telling me why you felt such urgency to come here today?"

I pressed my lips together, trying to suppress the urge of my fingers to tap away at my sides, and then sighed, trying to expel the tension from my body.

"I heard something today, something that no one else heard," I said. "It was a message on the PA system at school. Everyone else heard the crackling, but I was the only one who heard whispering."

It sounded ridiculous. And kind of scary. Right out of a horror movie, actually. Add some creepy music and a vertigo effect, and tada—terrifying.

"It said something like …" I furrowed my brows, trying to remember the exact words. "Give it back, Chosen One." I shrugged helplessly. "But it wasn't real. No one else heard it. So it's my mind playing tricks on me again. Doc, am I going crazy?"

I twisted my head, trying to look at her, but she seemed to be sitting slightly farther away from the couch than normally, and all I could get into view was her knee.

"It's possible that your mind is imposing parts of your dream onto reality because it's still dealing with your trauma, both in a physical and mental sense," she said.

"In a physical sense?" Frowning, I tensed different parts of my body to see if any of them were aching. But my injuries had healed a long time ago, and after rehab and just living life, I felt like I was basically back to normal. Maybe a little weaker because I hadn't rebuilt all the muscle mass I'd lost, but close enough.

"You were in a coma for three months during a time when your brain is still developing. A traumatic injury like yours can have a severe impact on your personality and cognitive functions. Some of it might heal over time, others you may need to learn to manage."

She was right. Of course she was. It was a miracle I was functioning as well as I was, even I knew that.

"You mentioned something like this happening before, with the monster you saw at the mall."

I nodded.

"Did it feel similar to you?"

"I guess so. Both felt threatening, like they were specifically targeting me."

"For now, let's go back to the voice. Did you recognize it?"

I tried to remember. It was hard to tell a voice from a whisper, but it hadn't sounded familiar from what I could tell. "I don't think so."

"And do you have any idea what it was referring to?"

I hesitated. "Well, the Chosen One is me, I guess, but I haven't the faintest idea what they want me to give back. In my dream I didn't take anything, and I haven't stolen anything in real life either."

"I see." She made some scribbles. "Why would you assume that the voice was accusing you of stealing instead of, say, borrowing something?"

Startled, I realized she was right. I had assumed that, but I wasn't sure why, either.

"I'm not sure," I said. "I guess there was something in the tone that sounded like it?"

"And have you had any other episodes of this nature?"

Episodes, she called it. As if it was some form of TV show.

"Not like this," I said. "But I still find myself listening out for weird sounds and movements when I'm in crowds. Sometimes I think I hear the clattering of swords."

She took some more notes.

Even though I was doing better, the world from my dream still seemed to linger at the edges of my consciousness, no matter which way I turned. Dr. Steinberg had made it clear to me that the healing process was going to take time. Possibly even years. But I wished I could hurry it up somehow.

"What do you do in those situations?"

"I look around to check, but the moment I look, the sound is gone."

The scratching of her pen on her notepad continued.

I sat up and turned properly so I could see her face. There were deeper lines in her frown than usual. What I was telling her was concerning her. Well, that was great news.

"Have you had any more visual episodes since that one time?"

"Usually in the evening. From the corner of my eye, I see a shadow move, with red eyes and fangs, but the same thing always happens … when I look at it properly, it's gone."

The lines softened a little. Then she put her notebook down. "This is completely confidential and will never leave this room, not even to your parents. Ben, I need to know, have you ever partaken in any mind-altering substances?"

She looked at me head-on, her gaze serious.

Blood rushed to my face.

"I smoked some weed a year ago," I confessed. "But I only had a few drags. I barely felt anything."

"And was weed the only substance you used?" Her gaze was intense, as if she was burrowing inside of my head to uncover my secrets.

I nodded. I'd never really had occasion, or interest, in trying anything else. Even weed hadn't really been my thing.

Dr. Steinberg smiled again. "That's good," she said. "Keep it that way. Using any substance right now could cause great detriment to your health and healing process. Don't jeopardize it for some kicks."

Somewhat intimidated, I gave her an awkward thumbs-up, and we returned to our normal session.

"How are you sleeping?" she asked. "Do you still have nightmares?"

"Every night."

"Then I'd like to talk to you about Phillip, today."

We'd been doing this for the past few sessions—going over my relationships with people from my dreams. We'd started with Tara and worked our way through most people I'd dreamed up. Today was Prince Phillip's turn. I was impressed with Dr. Steinberg for remembering all the names of my imaginary friends. She must have made a list for herself somewhere to keep up with it.

With each relationship, she helped me draw connections between qualities that I admired about them and qualities that I desired I had. Sometimes she helped me to see how I'd projected a certain image or feeling onto those people. It was a real eye-opening experience.

Finally, she set down her notebook.

"We've done great progress today," she said and smiled. She almost always said that, though, so I didn't put too much stock into it.

"Now to a slightly more serious subject though," she continued. "From what I can tell, you're experiencing anxiety induced by mild schizophrenic episodes, probably caused by your trauma, which may be aggravated by a hypersensitivity to external stimuli."

She paused to let her words sink in. I wasn't sure what to say. Did I need to say anything?

"Right now, it's too early to tell if this is a temporary state, or if your brain has taken permanent damage, so we will need to keep an eye on it. I will need to inform your parents, but I will be happy to answer any questions they or you may have over the phone as well."

She handed me a page from her notepad, fixed with a stamp.

I couldn't even make out any part of the writing on it.

"This is a referral to get you another brain scan for safety, and this is for some medication that should help bring these episodes under control for the time being. That being said, I'd like to commend you on how you've been dealing with them. You've taken a very rational approach, which is the best thing you can do with this."

Schizophrenia, huh? I hadn't expected that. It did, however, give me an explanation for the weird stuff that I'd been hearing. I just hoped it was a temporary issue, not a permanent one.

I stopped by the pharmacy on my way home from school the next day. I only told Mom about the brain scan and that I had been prescribed some medication, but not why. I didn't want to worry her with something like schizophrenia. An uncle of hers had suffered from something like it, and I didn't want to add more to the mountain of anxiety I had already created for her. Besides, I was certain that Dr Steinberg would do a much better job of explaining the situation than I could do.

Sitting in my room with the medication, I looked over it, reading the instructions and inspecting it dubiously. There were three things—two separate pills, and one drop. At least one of the pills was for anxiety, but I wasn't quite sure what the other two were, even after reading the instructions. One of them was meant to regulate certain hormones, and the other … I didn't get it.

But what was important was that it was going to make me better, right?

So I took them all in the prescribed doses.

I only needed to take them twice a day, once in the morning, once in the evening. That was manageable without letting anyone know.

I started taking them regularly, never missing a single dosage.

Wednesday, I realized I had forgotten half my books for my classes in my locker, instead taking the wrong ones to my classes. Thursday the same thing happened, plus I left some of my homework on my desk at home. In the afternoon, during my MMA training, I felt slower, more sluggish, and Jack beat me with ease. His hair was now forest green in color, though I barely had enough presence of mind to comment on it.

"What's up with you?" he asked, grinning cockily. "Your head's not in the game, huh? Got girls on the brain?"

I shook my head, as much to negate his assumption as to clear it up. A haze had settled in and I neither liked it, nor could I get rid of it.

"New meds," I said, figuring that would be

enough information to get him to lay off me. It was.

He just clapped my back sympathetically. "Got it. Hope you get used to them soon."

I didn't want to get used to them. Getting used to them meant accepting this hazy state of a half-working brain. I didn't like it, but I didn't have enough presence of mind to think of doing something about it.

By Friday, I'd almost forgotten about the rally I'd promised to watch, but luckily Harvey caught me just as I was unlocking my bike, and dragged me over to the pitch.

The cheer squad was great, Vivienne in particular, but I could barely appreciate it.

I waved back to her when she passed me with the rest of the troupe, but there was no chance to chat. It was for the best. I was getting tired much quicker with this medication and my eyes were already starting to droop.

I kept up with the regular doses day after day, despite the way it impacted my focus and attention. My head constantly felt like it was wrapped in cotton, and I found it difficult to focus. Even my emotional state was more subdued, though Dr. Steinberg told me that was normal during my adjustment period. She said that my body would get used to dealing with the medicine after a while, and while some side effects might remain, others would subside with time.

Since it definitely helped my paranoia and any audiovisual hallucinations I might have had, I kept it up.At least until the night before the escape room during spring break.

I wanted to have a clear head for the next day, and missing it for just one day wouldn't kill me, right? I could get used to it afterward. I was sure it'd be fine.

I didn't take it the next morning either, my mind already clearing up again. For the first time in a few weeks, I was actually starting to feel excited again, and a smile came to my face as I thought about the escape room in the afternoon. It'd be a blast!

CHAPTER 9

Jack and David collected me before picking up Vivienne as well, which allowed me to make the introductions before we got to the venue. For the first time in a long time, I cursed about not having a car yet. It usually wasn't that big a deal in Mitchell's Creek — everything was in cycling distance, and I liked the exercise — but when picking up a girl for a date, however casual it might be, it would have been nice to do it in my own car.

My only relief was that Jack was in the same boat as I was. He relied on David to drive because he didn't even have his license yet.

We soon arrived at the escape room, where Harvey was already waiting with Cindy. Those two had managed to get really close, really quickly, but apparently, they still weren't dating, at least not officially.

Apparently, Jack had booked us into the facility's *Couple's Special*. It involved each couple being locked up separately and they had to work together to get to the main room, where everyone would meet and then work together as a larger team to complete the final puzzles. It meant that it was also possible for only a few of the participants to win. Apparently, a lot of couples never made it out of the first room. The emphasis the attendant put on letting us know that there were cameras in each room that would be watching the players made me laugh.

I was intrigued by the setup, and there was an unspoken agreement between Jack, Harvey, and me that this was not only a joint effort to escape … oh no, it was also a competition to see who'd make it to the main room first. In this competition there were no stakes—if only because it would have been awkward to discuss them in front of our respective dates.

Soon, we were locked in. Vivienne and I glanced at one another, grinning.

"So, where do we start?" I asked, inspecting our surroundings around a little dumbly.

The room appeared like an old-timey study, along with a wooden desk, bookshelves on every wall, and a globe on a stand. Vivienne looked around the room critically, and then pointed to a framed painting of a mountainous landscape underneath a rainbow on the wall behind the desk. "Let's check if there's anything behind it."

I shrugged. It was as good a place as any to start. I reached up to get it down for her, and she opened the back of the frame. She was right—there was a plasticized piece of paper in the back, with some sort of code.

I stared at it. "Kinda looks like coordinates to me."

She turned to me, beaming. "That's it!"

I followed her over to the globe on the stand, and poked at it, only to realize that the metal ring around it could be moved. There was a pin at one point on the ring which we moved to the coordinates we'd discovered.

With a click, the globe opened like a hidden drink cabinet. And just like one might have expected, it was filled with spirit bottles, though I didn't doubt that these were only tinted bottles filled with water. There was nothing else, not even in the top half of the cabinet.

We glanced at each other, neither of us with a suggestion on what we should do with them.

Vivienne shrugged. "Keep searching, I guess."

So we did.

While I went to search around the table, she tested out the books on the shelf.

The drawers were full with fake handwritten letters, ink, quill, and parchment, some of which had clearly been signed by previous visitors with imaginative lines such as *Hailey & Carl 4eva* and *K+M* and *Rosa waz here*, but nothing of use.

I crouched underneath the table, where I found an unexpected keyhole on the table's underside.

Almost at the same time, Vivienne shouted out, "I've got something!"

I looked up, and she showed me a book that

had been hollowed out, now holding an wrought-iron key.

"Great job!"

After grabbing the key, I ducked back underneath the table, turning it in the lock. A little compartment came free, and I drew it out. In it was a parchment with a riddle.

"Rainbows make the world go round,
And sometimes help a path be found."

I stared at the nonsense.

"What does that mean?" Vivienne asked, confused.

I shook my head, as baffled by the clue as she was.

Closing my eyes, I tried to remember every detail of the room we'd seen so far. Then it hit me.

"The drink cabinet! The lids are all different colors!"

Vivienne jumped up and started rearranging the drinks.

"This one can't be moved," she said, pointing at the one with the purple lid.

Crap. What order did the colors in a rainbow go again?

But I needn't have worried. Vivienne was already at it, rearranging the bottles meticulously. We looked around, expecting something to happen, but nothing did. I looked at the colors, wondering if she'd arranged them wrong, but no, even when I went over it in my head, I was sure it was right.

"Maybe the other way?" she suggested and rearranged the bottles again.

Nothing.

I wracked my brain. There had to be something we'd missed …

The painting.

There'd been a rainbow on it, but different to this one somehow. I hadn't paid it a lot of attention earlier, but it must be connected. I picked up the frame we'd left sitting on the desk and turned it around.

"The order is different," I muttered, and then showed Vivienne. "It's different. I think we have to use this order!"

She'd done it before I'd even finished my sentence, switching around red, blue, and green. This time, there was an audible click from the bookshelves. We shared a glance and headed for it, trying to push it aside. It moved easily, revealing another room.

"That was easy," I said, grinning. And by the looks of it, neither of the other two teams had made it here yet.

This room was completely different. It looked like a massive laboratory, the kind a crazy scientist would have been proud of, locked by a large, heavy metal door. And over the door was a countdown. We had about forty-five minutes left to figure out how to open it. Fifteen minutes in the previous room was all we'd needed.

It must have been around this time when my medication fully left my system.

As we surveyed the room, testing for secret hints and compartments, I started feeling weird. Weird in the way that I would have described as sensing the presence of Corrupted Ones before. Now, I recognized it as vague, undirected anxiety. I felt like there were things in the shadows of the dimly lit room watching me. Waiting for me to make a mistake and step closer, so they could snatch me up and tear me to shreds.

Shadows moved when they shouldn't, but when I whirled toward them, I found nothing. While Vivienne searched for clues, I was preoccupied by trying to prove to my brain that there was nothing here to worry about.

My head wouldn't listen to reason. It screamed at me to get out, to run while I still had a chance, or to at least grab a weapon. So I did.

I went back to the study, and grabbed a letter opener which, while still completely blunt, was the closest thing to a weapon I could get my hands on.

"What are you doing?" Vivienne asked, peeking in on me in the study.

I turned to force a smile at her. "I have a gut feeling that this might be a clue of some sort."

"Nice!"

She accepted my lie readily, smiling brightly at me, and went back to search for further clues. I felt less vulnerable with the letter opener, but my mind was far more occupied with potential threats jumping out at us than figuring out clues. Still, Vivienne managed to figure it out quickly, with very little input from me, and we soon managed to open the door.

The attendant strolled toward us with a big grin.

"I think you guys might have just set a new record!"

He handed each one of us a certificate. With our time on it, both overall, as well as for the first room. He peeked into the room.

"But it looks like your friends are gonna be a while." He shook his head in mild exasperation. "I swear, it's like people forget that we have cameras in there for safety the moment the doors close."

I didn't even want to think about what sorts of things they'd been forced to watch in this couple's exercise, but I could imagine well enough.

"But I have to ask," he turned to me, "why did you think the letter opener was going to be relevant? It's the first time anyone's ever grabbed that after they'd entered the second room."

Desperate to come up with a believable story quickly, I shrugged and handed it back to him. "I figured maybe some clue might be hidden in a narrow spot that we'd need a tool for."

It was lame as far as excuses went, but the guy accepted it nonetheless.

My anxiety was fading now that we'd left the confines of the rooms, but I still wasn't able to fully relax.

Vivienne grabbed my hand. "They have a café by the waiting area. Wanna go there until they make it out?" She indicated the room behind us.

"Yeah, sounds good."

Having her take my hand felt weirdly good. Reassuring. It confirmed that I wasn't alone, and helped to dispel some of my demons. I looked at her as she led me to the café, like, really looked at her, as if I was seeing her for the first time.

She wore her hair free today, allowing it to cascade over her shoulders in loose, blonde curls. The only other time I'd ever seen it down was when we'd gone to the movies. It was pretty. Completely different to anything I'd thought my type was, but ... very pretty.

Her outfit was cute, too. Boots with a miniskirt and a ruffly top.

After we ordered sodas and sat down, she, in turn, watched me for a moment.

"You know," she said, "you seemed a little on edge in there. Are you okay?"

I glanced at her. So she'd noticed. I'd hoped she wouldn't.

"I'm fine," I lied. "But thanks for worrying."

Her eyes were still fixed on me. "It's just ... Harvey told me a little about what's going on with you."

Anger boiled up in my stomach. Damn that Harvey. He shouldn't talk about this to other people. That was *my* business.

"It was right after you turned me down," she continued.

My anger simmered out a little. Harvey *had* mentioned to me that he'd "fixed" my situation with Vivienne by explaining a little to her. It had actually helped me a lot after I'd realized I'd been holding on to a fantasy. I guessed I could forgive him this once. He'd only been trying to be a good friend.

"And he said that you get nervous a lot, and that you're still dealing with things you experienced in your ... after your accident."

She looked up at me with big, blue eyes, and my anger completely dissipated. This conversation would have happened sooner or later, right? Might as well get it out of the way. I sighed.

"Yeah, I'm still dealing with it. I've started taking meds that are meant to help, but I didn't take them today because I wanted my head to be clear. I wanted to have fun today."

A sympathetic smile appeared on her lips, and she grabbed my hand.

"You should keep taking it if it helps you. Maybe some day you won't need them anymore, but for the moment, you should do everything you can to get better. We'll all support you every step of the way, you know that, right?"

I nodded, though I wondered who exactly "we all" was in her eyes. I sighed. Then I gave her a crooked grin and squeezed her hand. "Wanna go out with someone who has mental issues?"

She blushed a little, but she didn't turn away. "If that someone is you, then yes."

"Can the medication make these 'episodes' worse?" I asked Dr. Steinberg.

She hesitated.

"In principle, they shouldn't. However, if you stopped taking them suddenly instead of slowly reducing the dosage, you might experience their sudden lack as a discomfort. In those cases, it could negatively impact your anxiety and it might spike."

So that's why the escape room day had been so bad.

I'd been taking my meds normally since then, accepting the grogginess and all, hoping that with time, it would go down a little. It hadn't yet.

"How have they been working for you now that you've been taking them for longer?" Dr. Steinberg asked, watching me.

"My head doesn't work right with them," I said, even though we'd already gone over that before. "And I feel tired all the time. I'm slower, too."

As if that was exactly what she'd expected to hear, she nodded. I supposed I was only repeating what I'd shared with her before.

"Any episodes?"

I told her about the escape room, and she chided me for stopping taking them.

"Medication like that doesn't work well if you treat it as a voluntary method. You have to stick to it. Think of it like antibiotics—you're actually risking it getting worse if you stop taking them before the treatment is completed."

I nodded, guiltily. I knew how bad things could get without them, and I really didn't want to experience it again.

"How long do you think the treatment will take?" I asked.

"We'll stick with the current dose for a few more weeks, then we can try reducing it slowly. If you adapt to the change well, we can speed it up a little."

A few weeks, huh? I hoped I'd be able to go on a lower dosage by the time we had planned to go to the carnival. I'd like to enjoy that to its fullest.

"I've been thinking about not participating in the MMA regionals this year," I confessed. "While I'm on the meds, I'm too slow. I can't fight well."

"Medically speaking, I think that's a good idea," she said. "Perhaps you should consider taking a break from training for a little while as well. Since fighting was such a big part of your dream, keeping it up might be reminding your brain of it."

I shot up, staring at her in disbelief. Giving up training? That was insane!

"I'm not suggesting stopping forever," she was quick to calm me. "And I'm also not saying to cut out any exercise. But perhaps you should focus on a different type ... something more relaxing and calming like Yoga, Tai-chi, or Capoeira."

I fell back, disappointed.

"Maybe," I grumbled.

I'd been doing MMA for years, since Dad signed me up because he figured it would be good for me to know some form of self-defense and help me build up some confidence. It had always been the first place in every new city where I'd been able to make friends. Giving it up out of nowhere, even if it was just for a while ... it felt like a big change. And I didn't like it one bit.

Chapter 10

I fell into a certain routine—I woke up, took my meds, went to school, went home. Then, on Mondays, I went to see Dr. Steinberg and told her about my week. Every other day I played computer games, or, when I had the energy, I practiced my drums. I hadn't picked up my lessons or band again after I'd woken up from my coma, and apparently, that's how it was going to stay for the moment.

Sometimes after school, I'd hang out with Vivienne and her friends at the mall. On the weekends, we usually did something together, but it was never anything big.

Taking my meds without exception meant that I was always a little drowsy, not quite on the ball. My schoolwork was definitely suffering, but Mom didn't mind. She said that was to be expected and it was a small price to pay for me getting better in the long run, even if it might mean repeating the year.

Then, finally, the day came when Dr. Steinberg told me we could lower the dose and see what that would do. This news actually managed to elicit a little excitement within me, in spite of the tranquilizing effect the meds had on me. Maybe I'd even be able to be a normal human with emotions and halfway intelligent thoughts again.

She prescribed me a significantly lower dosage, but it was far from nothing, and the change came gradually. The first day, I started having clearer thoughts again. Only a few, but it was better than nothing. The second day, the constant drowsiness faded. The third day, I was actually feeling excited about seeing Vivienne. The fourth day, I decided it was time to introduce her to my parents.

I knew they'd be over the moon. After all, it was the first real-life girlfriend I'd had. As far as they were concerned, it was a big deal. And, well, considering how pretty and nice she was, I felt pretty lucky. I still had no idea why she liked me, but it didn't matter. All that mattered was that she did, accepting my flaws and my current situation completely without reservation. It was awesome. *She* was awesome. And I had no doubt that my parents would share that view.

When I told Vivienne about my idea on Friday in school, she jumped in excitement.

"Oh my gosh, yes! Oh, but what should I bring? I have to give them something, right? What kind of thing do they like? Wine? Chocolate? Oh, I know! I can bake carrot cake for them! Do they like carrot cake?"

Her excitement was contagious, and I laughed.

"Okay, first of all, calm down? And whatever you bring them, they'll love it, I'm sure."

"Well, you're no help," she pouted, and I leaned forward to kiss her forehead.

"You don't need my help. You're perfect as is."

So I was a romantic, what of it? Sue me.

Step one—invite girlfriend for dinner Saturday—check.

Step two—tell the parents they will meet girlfriend for dinner Saturday.

"Hey, Mom," I called when I got home. I knew she only had a half day on Fridays, so she was always home when I got there.

"Yes, honey?" She was in the garden, watering the slowly dying plants, which was no surprise, as it had been a dry spell for the past few weeks.

"Hey, so, mind if I have someone over for dinner with us tomorrow?"

She looked up, a soft smile brightening her features. The dark rings under her eyes that had been so prominent for the first months after I had woken up again were almost gone. There were still traces, but I could only see them when I was looking for them. It was a relief to see the change in her.

"Sure. Is it Jack or Harvey?"

Ouch. Assuming I only had two friends who might come over, was she? Although when I thought about it, she wasn't all that wrong. There really was no one else I would even consider inviting. Aside from Vivienne, of course.

I shook my head. "It's my girlfriend. I figured it might be nice since dad's home and all."

She had the exact reaction I'd expected. "Girlfriend?" She lowered the watering can slowly and her face went from surprise into a beaming smile in no time. "Absolutely! What does she like to eat? Is she vegetarian? Vegan? Fussy about anything? Does she have any allergies? What kind of dessert does she like? I could make crème brûlée, does she like that kind of thing?"

It struck me how similar their reactions were to one another. It was almost a little creepy. *Like they're the same person but decades apart. Ugh.* That was a gross thought. *No, thank you.*

I deliberately shoved that thought far, far away and focused on Mom's questions instead.

"She eats pretty much anything. I'm sure whatever you decide to make will be great. You don't have to go fancy or anything."

She nodded absent-mindedly, and I wondered if she'd heard even a word of what I'd said. She was probably already planning a five-course meal and a show to top it off. I could only hope that she was more level-headed when she actually met her.

"Her name's Vivienne, by the way."

"Vivienne." She smiled. "What a lovely name."

Leave it to Mom to obsess over what the girl

would or wouldn't eat and completely forget to ask her name.

Saturday came and Vivienne — all dressed up, but in a tasteful way — showed up exactly on time, a Victoria sponge cake in a plastic tub under her arm, along with pralines and a bottle of wine.

"You went way overboard," I whispered, grinning, as I let her in and took her coat.

She shrugged helplessly. "I couldn't decide which was best. Do you think they'll like it?"

Looking hopeful, she raised her arms of gifts. I suppressed a chuckle. "Don't worry so much, it'll be fine. Really, I should be the one worried about meeting *your* parents, not the other way around."

I led her to the living room, where Dad was theatrically reading a book, and Mom was still busy in the kitchen.

As we entered, Dad put the book down and rose to his feet.

"Ah, you must be Vivienne," he said, reaching out to shake her hand.

Gently, I mouthed to him, and he gave me an almost imperceptible nod before taking Vivienne's hand. I'd warned him ahead of time not to squeeze too hard — he could have a real death grip when he didn't think about it, and he once told me how he broke a poor guy's hand just trying to greet him.

Mom bustled out of the kitchen, all smiles and housewife vibes. "Vivienne." She rounded the table with open arms. "Ben's told us so much about you!"

She hugged her, only to guide her to a seat, and I had to cover up my laugh with a cough. Yeah. Told them so much. Since yesterday. Right. Although admittedly, Mom had been badgering me with questions all day.

"Dinner's almost ready. Why don't you sit here and talk with my husband for a moment. Ben, would you be a dear and come help me?"

Knowing her overly sweet tone of voice too well, I knew I had no choice in the matter. I gave Vivienne an apologetic smile and met Mom in the kitchen.

Safely behind the walls, Mom turned to me and widened her eyes.

"She's so pretty!" she whispered.

Oh, Mom, really? You want to do this now?

"I know." I grinned. "She's smart, too. But you'll need to have an actual conversation with her to notice that."

"I know, I know." She grabbed some of the pots standing on the stove. "Here, take this in."

I helped her serve the food, and before long, dinner was in full swing. By the time we had Vivienne's cake for dessert, she was already joking around with my parents as if they'd known each other for months, even years. Mom's expression, a mix of wonder and pleasure, told me all I needed to know about how she felt. She was impressed, though whether it was with Vivienne, or with me for getting a girlfriend as amazing as her, I really couldn't guess. Dad was better at guarding his expression, but not good enough for his son to fail noticing the way he engaged in the conversation. Vivienne had completely and utterly won over my parents.

"So how did you two meet?" Mom eventually asked, the desire to know more sparkling in her eyes. She'd posed me the same question before, but I hadn't been able to provide her with a satisfying answer. Apparently "School" was not elaborate enough for the woman.

Vivienne glanced at me and smiled softly, her gaze briefly flitting to my chest, where the ring she'd given me took a prominent place above my shirt.

"It was about a year ago, actually." She looked back at my parents, her voice gentle. "I was having a horrible week. We'd lost the cheer offs and I'd twisted my ankle during it so I couldn't train to let out all that pent-up frustration." She shrugged and chuckled.

All three of us were spellbound by her story.

"I was feeling sorry for myself afterward, sitting on the bleachers in the rain when Ben walked by. He came up to me, and gave me a ring before telling me, *You did great. Chin up, there's always a tomorrow.*"

My hand flew to the ring around my neck when Vivienne looked back at me, and she smiled. *There's always a tomorrow.* No wonder she had returned it to me in the hospital.

Now that she'd told the story, I did actually remember. I hadn't really known it was Vivienne at the time, but Harvey and I had watched the cheer offs, or part of it anyways, and afterward, I'd seen a forlorn cheerleader. I'd felt bad for her, and so I gave her the ring I'd found on the bleachers earlier that day. It had held no special meaning to me, and so it had never imprinted on my memory.

Harvey had been with me at the time, even though I'd gone up to her on my own and he had made fun of me after, talking about how I was proposing to cheerleaders I'd never even spoken to before now.

Vivienne blushed. "It took me a while to gather my courage to speak to him after that, but he helped me a lot that day, and I remember it any time I'm feeling down about myself."

Grateful that I finally knew our origin and touched that my impulse had meant so much to her, I leaned over and squeezed her hand.

"You know, we actually met in quite a similar way," Dad said, waggling his eyebrows. "Although our roles were reversed compared to yours."

He then launched into the story of how my parents had met and the conversation took a natural flow from there until we'd had dessert, coffee, and a little break to let everything settle.

"Do you think I did okay?" Vivienne gnawed on her lip nervously as I brought her to the door and handed her the coat from the rack. "I was terrified the entire time of saying the wrong thing!"

I laughed and kissed her. "You did great. They couldn't possibly have loved you more."

Sighing, smiled. "That's a relief. Thank you for this, Ben."

She reached up and kissed me back, before jumping off into the night to her car.

Shaking my head at her, I closed the door. I felt like I should be the one thanking her, not the other way around. My parents were still sitting at the dining table, watching me as I came back inside.

"Yeah?" I asked, trying to give them the opportunity to say whatever it was they were so desperately failing to hide.

"You pick 'em well, champ," was all my dad had to say.

Mom was a lot more wordy in her praise. "She's delightful! So pretty, and good manners, and all in all lovely …"

I grinned. "Yeah, I'm pretty lucky."

"Don't forget that girl also has a good brain in

that pretty head of hers," Dad added, and Mom nodded vehemently.

"She does! Why don't we invite her to game night some time? I'm sure it'd be a lot of fun."

I contemplated Mom's suggestion for a moment. It might be nice. Vivienne would fit right in. But I had a feeling I should meet her parents before that happened. Quid pro quo and all that.

CHAPTER 11

I didn't know what it was about this level of medication, but it seemed the perfect amount for me — I could think clearly, deal with my daily life, and it still kept my demons at bay. I didn't even have nightmares anymore. I felt like I'd left everything Halastaesian behind, now finally able to deal with life for real.

If I didn't fear another anxiety relapse like I'd had at the escape room, I would have gone off the meds entirely, thinking I was cured. But I was far too aware that my current state of bliss was largely thanks to their effects. I wasn't about to take that for granted.

The carnival came to town and started setting up. Everyone in our group was excited for our plan to see the fireworks and then enjoy the opening night to its fullest. It would be completely overcrowded, but I didn't mind. With my medication, I was no longer trying to listen to every sound around me. It no longer put me on edge as much as it had, so even being in a crowd should be fine.

Something about the excitement coming up to

the day must have had a bigger effect on me than I'd realized, because the night before the carnival, I had another nightmare for the first time since going on medication.

Tara, Ronan, and Phillip sat in a circle, candles on the ground between each of them, and then one larger one in the middle. Each of them had an item sitting on the ground in front of them. Tara had my ring, Ronan had the bridle from my horse, and Phillip had my sword. I was looking at them from above, only wondering what they were doing. If I hadn't known any better, I'd have thought they were holding a memorial in my honor.

Then, Tara's eyes shot up. The dark circles underneath them, much like my mom's a few months ago, stood out from her pale expression.

"Ben!" she shouted.

The other two looked up as well—Ronan surprised, Phillip smug.

"Finally."

"Wow, can't believe it actually worked," Ronan muttered. "Yo, bud, you wanna come down here?"

I could do little more than stare at them. They looked older than I'd left them, tired. Then, dark shadows encroached on them from all sides and one candle after another was blown out by gusts of wind I couldn't feel.

"No!" Tara screamed and whirled around as colors faded into monochrome. Something jumped at her from the shadows—a Corrupted One. She drew her sword and blocked its attack, trying to fight back with long slashes so characteristic for her. Before long, Ronan and Phillip each had to fight one of them, too. Unfortunately, more appeared in the shadows. And sprinkled among them … Silver cloaks.

Another candle was blown out.

Phillip looked up at me, glaring. "It's not over. Far from it. You need to get your ass back here, or they'll be coming for you there."

His voice faded into static as the next candle extinguished.

One of the Corrupted Ones noticed me, and just as I saw its brethren overpower my friends, it lunged at me.

The final candle flickered and went out.

Gasping for air and clutching my chest where I'd expected the claw's impact, I jumped up in bed.

Eyes wide, I jerked my head around my starlit room, but found no monsters, no candles— nothing. My entire body was flush with adrenaline, ready to fight. Calming my breathing and forcing my muscles to relax, I turned on every light I could find.

What a weird and horrible dream. Staring at the box with my meds, I contemplated whether I'd forgotten to take a dose.

Nope, everything was as it should be. The compartment for the previous day was empty, the one marked for tomorrow or rather—as I noticed with a glance at my clock—today, still filled.

My heart was still beating like a drum. This nightmare was likely going to have me on edge all day, and it sucked that it was today of all days. Talk about bad timing.

I trudged to the bathroom, but the overhead light refused to turn on, leaving me in the dark. Determined to not let such a small detail affect me, I splashed my face in the sink, had a few gulps of water, and just leaned over the tap for a moment.

Suddenly, the light flickered on and off. Surprised, I blinked up at it but caught my own reflection in the mirror, looking like a ghost. I did a double take at the startled rush of adrenaline that was caused by noticing the dark shadow looming over me from behind. Whirling around, I found no more than an empty room, though the light was still flickering. When glancing at the mirror again, only my reflection stared back at me.

My mind was playing tricks on me again. It had to be that. I'd need to talk to Dr. Steinberg about increasing my dosage after all. Perhaps my body was getting too used to the medication, or else it just wasn't high enough to deal with the brain damage I might have. *Great*.

I glanced at the clock on my way back to bed. Five a.m. There was no way I was going to be able to get back to sleep, and it was too early to do anything else.

What had Dr. Steinberg told me to do instead of MMA again? Yoga? That was basically just meditation or something, right? Might as well give it a shot. I closed my eyes, sitting on the floor with crossed legs.

How did one meditate, anyway? I opened my eyes again and grabbed my phone to look it up online.

I found three different how-to-guides, but all of them seemed fundamentally different. And stupid.

This was so dumb. It was only a dream. Not even an imaginative one. It was about fictional people getting attacked by fictional creatures. Now, if Vivienne had been in the mix, it'd be different. Or Jack or Harvey. Hell, even Lauren and Rod would have made a difference. Because they were real. Way scarier.

And yet, despite my reasoning, I couldn't get the shaking out of my bones.

My paranoia was coming back with a vengeance, huh?

I decided to focus on another piece of Dr. Steinberg's advice and recorded the dream in my journal. Even as I wrote it down, I gulped. It was uncanny how many details I could remember. It was as easy as recollecting a memory from moments ago. Normally I found it much harder to get a hold of my dreams after I'd woken up—especially after I'd been up for a while.

I glanced at the clock. Coming up on six a.m. My skin was still crawling with the memory. At least it was now late enough that it wasn't completely unreasonable to be up.

Tired and on edge, I went down to the kitchen. Some kind of hot drink to warm me up would be a good call. I looked through the cabinets trying to decide. Coffee—no, I was already jittery enough. Tea—that was for old and sick people. Hot chocolate—well, it was the only option left, so it would have to do. It was even the fancy kind, with real chocolate. I heated up some milk in the microwave, checking it every ten seconds or so to stop it from bubbling over.

When it was done, I grabbed it, dropped the chocolate into it, and sat down in front of the TV to watch Saturday morning cartoons. Thank god children were notorious for being up early, or I'd have to deal with something serious. But seeing cartoon characters bump each other over the head with pianos, and still sort of remain friendly … well, that was just what I needed right now. I watched cartoon after cartoon, and soon, I felt my shoulders relax again. It had been nothing more than a dream.

A few hours later, Mom came bumbling down the stairs. She was halfway through the process of making coffee before she even noticed the TV was on.

"Oh! Morning, honey," she said, and yawned. "You're up early."

She plopped down on the couch next to me. "I thought I'd have to kick you out of bed around noon."

I shrugged. "Couldn't sleep anymore."

She nodded, as though she understood the issue all too well. Maybe she did.

"Mom." I muted the TV and turned to her. "Have you ever had a nightmare that was so realistic that you woke up and wondered if it was real? And then saw something from your dream around? Like a person or something."

She watched me quietly for a moment, but then she nodded.

"After your grandfather died, I had a lot of dreams like that. Reliving it, experiencing the aftermath … Sometimes with other people who weren't involved. And then when I woke up, I'd call them up, scared to hear that they'd died. Sometimes, I'd see your grandpa's reflection behind me in the mirror or thought I could smell him in my room."

Something about the way she looked at me when she spoke told me that she'd experienced it again after that accident, with me.

It wasn't a new story, and far from surprising. My grandpa had died in a car crash before I'd been born, and Mom had been in the car with him, but unlike him, she'd survived. Barely. I didn't know too many details, but apparently, it'd been quite a gruesome scene. And after my accident … It really wasn't surprising.

It reassured me to know that she'd experienced similar things to me after going through trauma, though.

She reached over and ruffled my hair before getting up again. "Let's have breakfast."

I was still a little riled up, but after I took my meds that morning, I felt better. I met up with Vivienne and the others in the late afternoon at the carnival's edge — we'd invited Jack and David as well. The carnival had opened around noon, and it was already bustling with people. We agreed that in case we got separated, we'd meet up for the fireworks by the corn on a cob stand.

We split into two groups — Rod and Harvey with Lauren and Cindy, and Jack and I with David and Vivienne. It was easier to move around in smaller groups, and we were interested in doing different stuff. The girls in the other group had wanted to get a layout of the carnival first, wanting to see what there was to offer, but Vivienne had insisted on going on a ride right away, and Jack had been all too eager to do the same.

I wouldn't have minded getting a feel for the

size of the carnival first, making a note of the layout and all, possibly due to old habits, dream or not, but I relented easily, just happy about how brightly Vivienne was beaming at me.

We stumbled from one attraction to the next, Vivienne always excited about the next thing she saw and needed to participate. The rest of us were dragged along, though I didn't get the impression that any of us minded. We went on rides, had snacks, played some games, watched a show, all the way until it was time to meet the others.

We met up at the agreed upon point—next to the corn on a cob stand—all ready with our snacks. Only moments later, the first bang lit up the sky in myriads of colors. The glimmers rained down from the sky, vanishing in the darkness before they ever reached the ground.

The shots came now in such rapidity, it reminded me of a thunderous drumroll, welcoming home the glorious heroes to Valhalla.

It was incredible, and my hand found Vivienne's while we watched. I glanced at her, her eyes sparkling as they reflected the spectacle in the sky … and suddenly my perception changed.

Tendrils of darkness reached up from the ground all around us —amongst all of the people from the crowd—rising higher like hungry vines, coalescing, until their shapes were all too obvious to me. They still remained only shadows—like a black, permeable mist, but panic rose in my chest nonetheless.

I tried to beat it down, tried to ignore what I saw, because I knew it wasn't real, but my eyes kept being drawn back to them. While being out here in the open didn't feel safe to me, none of the shadows seemed to be heading my way. In fact, the longer I watched them, the more I got the impression that they were wandering aimlessly.

"Ben? Are you okay?" Vivienne's voice reached me between the thunderclaps of the fireworks, and I finally looked at her again, realizing how tightly I was clasping her hand. Guiltily, I let up a little. I'd probably been hurting her.

"Sorry," I mumbled, though there was no way she could hear me. "I'm good."

She was still looking at me, her concern evident, and I put on a grin before gently moving her chin, so she was looking at the fireworks once more. She giggled.

When I looked around again, there were still shadows, but fewer. None of them were coming for me.

Even though I knew they were only figments of my imagination, Vivienne felt like a lucky charm to me, like a barrier against evil that kept the Corrupted Ones from noticing me.

I returned my gaze to the sky, determined not to let my brain ruin my night. The finale of the fireworks began and the pyrotechnics had done their job well — they painted a large wheel into the sky which looked enough like a Ferris wheel to elicit "ooh"s and "aaah"s from the crowd.

Then … darkness. For a moment at least. Gradually, the lanterns around the carnival flickered back on, and we were raring to continue our evening of fun.

"Let's do the haunted house," Harvey suggested. "They always work best at night anyway."

"I don't know," Lauren said with a glance at Rod. "They always have these stupid animatronic figures at these kind of things, and they're just … so lame."

"I think it'll be fun!" Vivienne turned to me. "Wanna go?"

I really wasn't sure how a haunted house would go with my ambiguous mental state, but faced with her obvious excitement, I couldn't bring myself to say that. "Sure."

In the end, only Harvey and Cindy joined us for the haunted house, the others preferring to go on the Ferris wheel to enjoy the lights from above.

We were sent in in groups of two by the somewhat bored looking middle-aged lady. Harvey and Cindy went in first, and we soon heard their first shouts of surprise.

When the lady jerked her thumb to tell us to head in, we wandered into the dark, curved tunnel that marked the haunted house's entrance. We'd made it about halfway, when the tunnel suddenly began flashing between bright lights and darkness, and clown jack-in-the-box heads jumped out at us from all sides.

Vivienne gave a squeak of scared surprise, clutching my arm for safety, and I gritted my teeth, trying not to tense my muscles. I'd never been a fan of jump scares. They were so cheap. And sadly so effective.

Adrenaline was shooting through my body, but I did my best not to show Vivienne my urge to run or fight. I wanted to be calm for her, so she felt safer.

We kept going, and a man with a chainsaw stepped out in front of us, revving the saw. It was clearly an actor, and he was chained to the wall, so we could squeeze past him without ever getting close to the chainsaw. However, his movements were less predictable than a figurines', and Vivienne stuck to me so closely, I found it difficult to walk.

"Not great with these kinda things, huh?" I asked her.

She shook her head silently, her eyes wide as she scanned our surroundings, trying to predict from whence the next terror would hail. Something dropped from the ceiling, landing on our heads, and I could tell almost immediately that they were only silk banner strings that were then pulled up again, but Vivienne screamed and dropped to the floor.

I knelt down next to her, and held her hand, trying to get her to look at me.

"Hey, Vivi, it's okay. I promise it's alright. There's nothing bad here, just you and me. Everything else is just actors and props. I'll keep you safe, okay?"

She looked at me, and nodded, slowly.

We continued walking.

I started hearing whispers. At first, I thought they were part of the attraction, something to unnerve us, but then I started listening to what they were saying.

"Chosen One … Give it back to us … Ben … Don't make us come to you …"

My heart pounded. I was pretty sure I'd heard a similar message before.

"Ben …"

"Why do they know your name?" Vivienne whispered to me.

As if struck by lightning, I stopped dead, staring at her.

"You can hear it?" I asked, incredulously.

She glanced around uncertainly. "Is this part of the show?"

Okay, no point in freaking out. She might not actually be hearing the same thing … right?

"Ben … Don't make us involve her … Chosen One … Give it back to us …"

My nerves lay bare. I grabbed Vivienne's hand as tightly as I could and ran, pulling her with me. I hoped to god this was just one of Harvey's pranks. I'd murder him if it was, but it would still be so much better than the alternative.

Vivienne shrieked suddenly, and I felt her pull back in my grip. I stopped running long enough to look back at her. Her face was a mask of terror and she pointed, her finger trembling, at the exit glowing up ahead. Almost instinctively, I followed her gaze.

I hadn't noticed it while we'd been running, but a shadow was rising from the ground, blocking our way out. A Corrupted One. And ... Vivienne could see it.

PART III

CHAPTER 12

Raising itself up, the Corrupted One turned to us and took a misty step forward, solidifying with every passing moment. Shielding Vivienne with my body, intent on protecting her with everything I had, I did a quick calculation to take stock of what my surroundings had to offer. There wasn't much. All I saw were props most likely made from plastic or cardboard and papier-mâché.

Gritting my teeth, I narrowed my eyes. I may have to do this old school. I wished I hadn't stopped training, but at least I wasn't completely out of shape.

I glanced at Vivienne and gave her a roguish smirk. I could do this.

"Stay put. I've got you."

She nodded ever so slightly, but it was all the assurance I needed.

The Corrupted One hadn't fully materialized yet, which limited my options. Its head, which would have been the best point of attack, was still a cluster of misty tendrils. Unfortunately, its claws were more present in a corporeal way — already digging into the dirt, leaving long gashes in their wake, proving they were just as sharp as I remembered them from Halastaesia.

I needed to wait for the right moment and use the adrenaline coursing through my body.

Watching the rate at which the Corrupted One's body stabilized, I held back just until the moment before its head finished coming into existence for real. My eyes glued to the backlit silhouette ahead of me, I sprinted toward it, ignoring the frightened gasp behind me. I dashed forward, evading its lazy slashes easily with a few sidewise leaps, ran one step up the wall to its left, jumped off, and grabbed its head just as I landed on its shoulders.

Holding onto its solid horns, I drove it straight into the other wall. I let go with one hand to pull my keys from my pocket, before plunging the longest one in its eye. It screamed in demonic outrage—a sound with a high enough pitch to shatter a crystal chandelier—and I jumped off its back. Dashing forward, I grabbed Vivienne's hand and dragged her with me, past the blinded and wild Corrupted One.

I pulled her with me through the calm, unsuspecting crowd until we'd reached the exit to the carnival, looking across the car park. Nothing there. We were safe for now.

"What ..." Vivienne gasped. "What was that?

And you …" She stared at me, horror reflected in her eyes. "How?"

Grimly, I met her gaze, trusting my other senses to warn me if another Corrupted One should approach.

I couldn't blame her for her reaction. Mine hadn't been that different the first time I'd encountered one of these monsters. But … I needed to be certain.

"Tell me exactly what you saw."

"What do you mean? You saw it too!" She turned half back to the carnival, as if to scan for the monster. "And you … that, that thing … *hic.*" She trailed off, the hiccups interrupting her scrambled thoughts.

I held her by her shoulders, forcing her to face me. "Please, Vivi, it's important."

I needed to know that she'd seen the same thing I had. That it really wasn't in my head.

After staring back at me blankly for a moment, her hiccups faded and she nodded, gulping. "That shadow came from the ground. And then it was a monster, with claws and teeth, and red eyes, and you …" She clapped her hands in front of her mouth, close to tears as she sank to the floor.

Time seemed to slow down as my blood ran cold.

Every beat of my heart brought another realization.

It was true.

The Corrupted Ones were real, and that meant…

That everything else was real, too.

I looked back to the carnival. There was no panic, no terror. All I could hear were the same sounds as before, of delighted laughter, maybe some joyful screams and shouts from some of the faster rides, accompanied by music. Either the Corrupted One had vanished the same way it had appeared, or it had been taken care of by someone else. If *they* could come through … why not someone else?

I thought of the nightmare with Tara, Phillip, and Ronan. Perhaps it had been no dream at all. The signs had been there this entire time … and I'd ignored them, thinking they were fantasy, illusions created by my mind.

"What is happening?"

Vivienne was crying now, her shoulders shaking as she rocked back and forth, huddled in a ball.

I knelt down next to her. This was going to be difficult for her to swallow.

"That was a Corrupted One," I told her. "They're creatures made from a heart filled with hatred in death and some other nasty stuff. And they're looking for me. You remember that whisper in the Haunted House? They were talking to me."

I shuddered as I remembered. They knew Vivienne was with me. They knew she was important to me.

"Remember my coma and what Harvey told you? About me having this dream where I was a hero fighting monsters? *Those* were the monsters. As it turns out, it wasn't just a dream after all."

I stood up and looked at her, miserable in fear.

"You need to go home," I said. "Now. I'll take care of this."

To my surprise, her shoulders calmed as she shook her head, wiping her tears away with one hand while taking mine with the other.

She stood up. "I can't let you go on your own. If something happened to you, I-I ..."

Her lips quivered, and I gave her a quick kiss.

"Okay, but you have to do *exactly* what I tell you, okay? And remember that it'll be dangerous."

I didn't have the time to argue with her, and maybe she could be useful. I couldn't be certain that *everyone* could see the Corrupted Ones. For all I knew she only did because she'd been touching me when it had appeared.

Determination was now taking the place of fear in her expression, though she still seemed a little jittery. Then again, who wouldn't moments after their first encounter with a supernatural threat?

We slowly headed back to the carnival, and I kept my eyes peeled for the Corrupted Ones and a weapon. Considering how many there'd been during the fireworks, they must be lingering all over the place, just waiting to activate until I got close. But what was it they wanted from me? I hadn't been able to bring anything back from Halastaesia. I didn't *have* anything.

What I wished I had was my sword. Then, it would be so easy to destroy them.

But I had to take what I could get. One of the first stalls we passed upon entering the carnival again was the rifling stand. I knew the bullets they used were a far cry from the real deal, but they might still help.

"You're a good shot, aren't you?" I asked Vivienne, remembering her near-perfect aim from earlier. I'd tried to show off and win her a cute toy, but she'd managed to get it on her own already. While she would probably not be able to best me in a sword fight, she was a better shot than I was, and she had her athleticism to boot.

I paused at the stand, and while the clerk was attending to another person, I grabbed one of the rifles and ran, Vivienne right behind me. We made it around a corner before he even noticed. I took off my trench coat and gave it to Vivienne along with the rifle. "Take this and hide it."

She nodded and put on the coat, keeping the air rifle inside, close to her body.

Next, I swiped some darts from a different stand, luckily without being spotted. While none of these would be enough to kill a Corrupted One, they could blind them, which would hopefully mean they'd retreat.

I waved for Vivienne to follow me, and we retraced our steps to the haunted house. I needed to check if it was still there.

Even though I had somewhat dilapidated the exit of the attraction, it looked like the monster itself was gone. Couple after laughing couple came out of it unperturbed.

But there were more. I could smell them.

Their stench was unmistakable. A hint of rotten flesh.

I surveyed our surroundings. Since I had no idea what exactly they were after, I had to make sure to contain their threat and deal with them now, while I had an idea about where they were. Besides, if they decided not to look for me anymore and just run wild here, hoping that I'd come to them instead … Well, a lot of lives were at stake. I sure as hell didn't want that on my conscience. Especially since some of those people were my friends.

I caught a whiff of a more intense trail.

"This way," I said to Vivienne and ran ahead, following the trail to the Ferris wheel. *Crap*.

The Corrupted One had just about finished fully materializing near the line by the time we got there.

"Duck," Vivienne shouted, and I did, though I continued running at the monster at full speed.

I heard two shots, and blood spurted from one of its eyes.

Nice aim, Vivi!

Rearing its head back, it let out a mighty roar — apparently the first catalyst for other people to notice its presence.

They twisted their heads trying to see where the sound had come from, but they didn't seem to see it. It was as though their attention just glossed over the giant monster in their paths.

While the Corrupted One was distracted, I grabbed the cord from the waiting line and closed the remaining distance between us. I leapt onto its back, clinging on to the spikes and tufts of fur. It whirled around, trying to throw me off, but I held on tightly. Another three shots, and the Corrupted One roared again.

Its second eye had been punctured. I used the brief reprieve in its thrashing to reach its neck and hauled the cord across it, and then around its muzzle, forcing it closed. Tying the rope to its horns as well as I could manage under strain, I then tried to direct it.

It broke into a panicked run.

Desperately, I pulled at the cord, trying to make it avoid people as best as possible. I was only grateful that the fireworks had marked the end of the night for a decent portion of the crowd, so there were less people around than before. Luckily, a monster charging at them was apparently something they *did* notice, and jumped aside, although their alarm didn't last for long.

I was planning on riding the Corrupted One outside and circling the carnival at a safe distance while trying to use it to get the attention of the others, so they'd leave the vicinity of people.

Turned out I didn't get the chance.

A young woman stayed rooted to the ground as the Corrupted One charged toward her, and no matter what I did, I couldn't get it to change direction anymore.

She lifted her hands, and green light flowed out gently, scooping underneath the Corrupted One and lifting it up.

Wait a minute. I know that spell!

Magic … worked here? Did that mean I could use magic again?

Imagining myself floating, I jumped off the monster's back. The ground met me with the usual firmness, but I managed to roll to absorb the impact. Nope, no magic for me.

I looked up at the woman who had taken care of the Corrupted One, and the breath caught in my throat. Her raven black hair was tied back to a ponytail, and she wore practical clothing, like she always did. Her large, expressive eyes were set on the Corrupted One, as she muttered another spell.

A moment later, the monster dissipated, and she let out a deep breath.

I was still staring but had managed to get to my feet. "Tara."

"No time for reunions, bud. Catch!"

No sooner had I heard Ronan's voice than I had a sword thrown to me. I caught it with ease. The familiar weight felt good in my hand. *Right.*

I had questions. So many questions. But Ronan was right—there was no time for that right now. There were more Corrupted Ones loose on the carnival grounds, and I was pretty sure I'd just heard screaming.

CHAPTER 13

Wasting no time, I rushed toward the source of the cry, and lo and behold! A Corrupted One had its claws around a teenager who … looked a lot like me. At the very least, we were roughly the same age and were wearing the same shirt. I silently apologized to him. That guy had the worst luck today.

I'd be a fool to cry out to get the Corrupted One's attention. Only heroes in movies would ever dream of doing that. In real life, you used every chance you could get, and if your opponent didn't know you were there, all the better. While the Corrupted One had its attention focused on my unfortunate lookalike, I stayed low, charging in from the side while using every piece of cover I could find. Then I jumped, stabbing it straight through the side into the heart.

There were a lot of ways to kill or banish a Corrupted One. Unfortunately, they had even more ways to kill you. And if you didn't receive any proper combat training, you'd be toast. So far, my body had moved on instinct alone, and I felt the increasing weight of my arms as I was tiring out more and more.

My lookalike dropped to the ground when the beast dissipated into nothingness. *Okay, good to know.* Kill the monster, it vanished from this world. That would certainly help when trying to avoid questions later. After all, you couldn't prove the existence of something that wasn't there.

I needed to fight smart. I could probably take down one or two more, but then I'd be pretty much powered out. Even now I doubted I could win a head-to-head fight. I was too tired already.

At least I was no longer alone on the battlefield. Tara and Ronan were here, too. And Vivienne.

Vivienne! Crap. I'd left her behind alone by the Ferris wheel.

Turning on the spot, I raced back to find her, garnering some confused looks from people I pushed past.

"Vivi!" I shouted through the crowds, hoping to get some answer.

My breath caught in my throat when I glanced up at the Ferris wheel. A large shadow was climbing up the center of the Ferris wheel even as it was in motion. *Seriously?*

Then I noticed a much smaller figure climbing nimbly ahead. Hastening my step, I clutched my sword tighter.

Vivienne. It had to be.

"Want a boost?" Suddenly Tara was running beside me, flashing me a grin.

My stomach did a loop-the-loop. Oh boy. There was something I was going to have to figure out later.

"Yes, please!"

She chanted a quick incantation as we kept running, and I could feel my legs get lighter. Then, it was like I received a massive wind boost from just underneath me, and I went flying through the air, onto the framework of the still moving Ferris wheel. I could feel it sway from side to side as I clung onto the painted metal. Its balance was all out of whack, and if any of us— including the monster—made one wrong move, it would tip over, probably severely injuring a bunch of people on the ride.

If only it would at least stop turning!

As though someone had heard my silent prayer, all of the carnival lights turned off, and along with it, the Ferris wheel's turning. Shouts and screams rose up everywhere as people found themselves disoriented, but I was glad the power had been cut, if only because it meant that I could move around more easily.

Sadly, it also meant I could no longer see very well. I knew Tara had flung me somewhere above the monster, and Vivienne had been climbing up on the other side.

The stench of rotting flesh was creeping into my nostrils with more intensity and, barely suppressing a sneeze, I looked down.

Oh hey, two glowing red eyes.

If that wasn't the perfect target to aim for, I didn't know what would be.

Letting go of my desperate hold to the Ferris wheel's framework, I stepped off, and aimed my sword directly for those eyes. Tara would catch me. As a fae, she had excellent night vision, and her magic was something quite literally out of this world.

My sword slid easily into the space between the monster's eyes, like a knife through warm butter. Satisfied, I smirked. It had lost none of its sharpness in my absence. Ronan must have taken good care of it in my stead.

A sound loud and high enough to make my eardrums throb erupted as the sword slid into the Corrupted One all the way to its hilt and it screamed in pain. I was still clinging onto it but was thrown around by the thrashing monster. The lights turned back on, as did the Ferris wheel's motion, causing the Corrupted One's hold on the Ferris wheel to slip. The monster dropped backward toward the ground in an impossibly slow arc, pulling me with it.

"Ben!" I heard Vivienne's terrified shout, but I couldn't deal with her right now. There's not much someone can do while they're falling, not even someone with my training. I could only hope that her shout was for my sake, and not because she found herself facing more danger.

Falling though we were, I still managed to pull my sword back out of the monster, though I didn't need to—the Corrupted One vanished into a fine black mist before it ever even came close to the ground.

As I'd hoped, Tara caught me with ease, her magic cushioning my fall so that I landed as softly as if I were wearing a parachute.

The moment I touched the ground, already searching for where the next monster was lurking, I heard Vivienne shout from high up. "Ben! The teacups!"

I glanced up to see her still clung onto the Ferris wheel and gave her a sharp nod before I took off running. Tara soon fell in step with me.

"Phillip is dealing with the perimeter, so we don't lose any," she said quickly. "Ronan is on the other side."

"How many have you guys dealt with already?"

"I'm not sure … maybe three or four each."

I grimaced to myself. I'd need to step up my game. Phillip would never let me hear the end of it if he ended up getting more of the beasties than I did.

The strangeness of that thought occurred to me suddenly, and warmth rushed through me. My friends were real, and they had come here to help me.

My memories were real, too.

My eyes slid to Tara as we ran, taking in her

fierceness, her dedication. She reminded me of the wind, running like this. Beautiful, too. A tremendous storm of flower petals and thorns who devastated her foes.

Suddenly, a Corrupted One jumped out in front of us, pinning down a young couple who screamed in fear. I had to do a double take, but there was no doubt … the couple cornered was Harvey and Cindy!

Before I could react, Tara had already done her thing.

Without even taking a break in her sprint, she mumbled a chant under her breath and reached out with her hands, violet energy forming between them, before shooting out at the Corrupted One like a lightning, impaling its torso. The creature dissipated before we even ran past.

I shot a glance at my friends as we did— Harvey had a scratch on the shoulder but that was all.

He happened to look up just in time, his face still a mask of terror, and our eyes met. Still, I couldn't stop. There were more monsters that needed taking out.

"Let's split up again," I panted, and Tara nodded before veering off. I hated how out of breath I was. Never again would I let my training slide, no matter what happened. Even if I woke up in yet another world straight out of some coma.

I headed toward the teacups, and indeed, a Corrupted One was spinning along on the plate with them, sniffing at the visitors.

I gritted my teeth. These things had always made me feel sick, and now I had to fight on one. At least it should be over quickly considering that I had my sword.

This monster had been noticed by a few people, and they were backing away from the carousel, though still not everyone seemed perturbed, including some of the people sitting in the teacups. I had to assume that they could in theory see it, but that their consciousness didn't pick up on it, much like the way in which a person might avoid walking into a streetlight without ever fully realizing it was there in the first place. And they continued not to notice until they had a reason to, either because it attacked, or because it was blocking off their way entirely. I assumed the same logic applied to me while I ran around the carnival, monster-slaying with my sword. Perhaps people might think it was a show of some sort. That would be a neat way to tie everything together.

I barged into the waiting line, leapt over the banister, and jumped straight onto the moving platform, ignoring the operator's affronted yelling. The sudden instability and movement of the ground took my balance, and I crashed into one of the teacups that held a group of people. Without giving them any more than a cursory glance, I pushed myself off again and made my way for the monster, making sure to keep my stance low and wide. It had noticed me now, a sly, grinning grimace forming on its monstrous visage as it turned to face me with a malicious glint in its eye.

If I'd needed any more proof that they were here for me, I'd gotten it now.

We eyed each other as the teacups went round.

"What are you doing, kid? Get away from that thing!" someone shouted behind me, but I paid them no mind.

I had a job to do.

Upon an invisible and inaudible command, I shot forward, staying low, dashing to its legs. Its tail came sweeping toward me, and I jumped, trying to avoid it. Unfortunately, I briefly forgot what we were fighting on, and the rotation of the teacup plate meant that I was struck anyway, square in the torso. The impact not only knocked the wind out of me, but also sent me sailing off the attraction and into a tent which collapsed over me. It took me a moment to recover and regain my breath—my body in this world wasn't used to taking hits of this magnitude—and it was enough time for the monster to cross over to me and fish me out of the tent's collapsed remains.

Next thing I knew, I was hanging in the air in the Corrupted One's grasp, and it was starting to take on a shadowy shape again. It was intentionally disappearing, probably intending to take me along.

I didn't hesitate to attack.

But I wasn't the only one.

While I slashed at its arm, Jack came running from the crowd, and jumped onto the creature's back, reached up to its head, around to its eyes, took a hold of its jagged and angled bones, yanked the head back and exposed the Corrupted One's throat, providing me with the opening I needed. With one smooth slash, I severed it, and both of us dropped to the ground as the monster vanished. I glanced at Jack.

"You alright?" I asked.

He nodded, though he did look a little freaked. Still, he'd been a real help to me.

"Thank you."

I looked around. We'd actually gained a little audience, and they all looked either terrified or worried. Most a mixture of both.

Welp. On to the next monster.

I left Jack behind, giving him time to recuperate, while I went off to search for the next. I heard the yells of people before I saw it, allowing me to follow it quickly.

A Corrupted One was tearing through a crowd, carelessly brushing people aside, occasionally peering at one of them up close. And oh, did the people notice this one! Most people ran away like headless chicken, but a few were frozen in fear, and even those who ran were struck by the monster.

I gritted my teeth. More monster slaying necessary.

But before I got a chance, a flash of silver appeared before me and disintegrated the monster. Then, the robed figure turned to me, their silver eyes looking me up and down with satisfaction.

CHAPTER 14

"Chosen One," the silver-banded mage said, offering his hand. "I am glad to have finally found you. You must come, quick, or your world is in peril."

Immediately trusting him, I reached out to the mage's hand. The silver-banded mages were the ones who had brought me to Halastaesia in the first place, so he was undoubtedly here to offer his assistance. They had helped me every step along the way in Halastaesia, and ultimately also sent me home.

An arrow pierced the mage's neck. Quickly another followed, impaling his shoulder, and a third went straight through his head. He dissipated into silvery dust before his body hit the ground, comparable to the way the Corrupted Ones vanished.

Trying not to be dumbstruck by the horrifying sight, I ducked and jerked around to find the archer, only to see Phillip running toward me, bow in hand.

"What the hell?" I yelled, but he only looked

past me with a grim expression, as if he were searching for his next target.

"Don't you dare trust a mage right now! I'll explain later."

Baffled, I didn't react.

Tara came running around the corner. "Oh good, you're together. I think we got all of them."

"Let's get out of here now, before people start asking questions," I suggested hastily, noticing the people nearby staring at the teenagers carrying lethal weapons. Some of the braver adults were already making their way toward us. Time to get out while we still had the chance. I had no desire to explain to anyone that supernatural creatures that I'd fought in my coma were now rampaging freely in this world.

I led our hurried escape from the carnival—not out to the car park, but into the fields on the far side to avoid the crowds. At some point along the way, Ronan joined us as well.

We stopped a little way out, far enough from the carnival lights that no one would immediately spot us, but close enough that we could keep an eye on the situation and return quickly if there were screaming or anything of the sort.

Now that we finally had a moment to breathe, Tara flung herself around my neck, squeezing me tightly.

"So, don't think I'm not happy to see you guys

or grateful for your help, but ..." I looked at them one by one as Tara let go of me. "Would any of you mind explaining what the hell is going on? How are you here? How are," I gestured toward the carnival, "*they* here?"

They exchanged a glance as if to silently determine who would explain, in which order, and how.

It seemed that Phillip drew the short straw.

He sighed exasperatedly.

"Look, we wouldn't have needed to come if you'd just started listening to what was around you. We tried to warn you, you know. It's not our fault you blocked yourself off from everything."

Ronan punched him in the shoulder with a warning look.

"What his royal haughtiness here means is that after you were sent back, things changed in Halastaesia. Well, not so much changed. More like we found out that what we *thought* was the truth, wasn't actually true. The dark prince was never the one pulling the strings."

"But then ..." I trailed off, my eyes widening.

Suddenly everything clicked into place. Why I'd been sent back so abruptly, why I'd seen flashes of silver amongst the monsters in my dream, why Phillip had killed the mage.

"The silver-banded mages?" I asked incredulously.

"Duh." Phillip watched me with a sneer. "Like

I said, we *tried* to warn you."

"They attempted to take Halastaesia over again from the shadows, but they hit a roadblock," Tara said quietly, watching me kindly. "They realized they need something they couldn't get anymore."

They all looked at me.

"Something I have."

She nodded, slowly. "I suspect it might be your magic. Or something like it, anyway. By coming to Halastaesia, you absorbed it, and when you returned here, it vanished. They think that it will return if you come back; if they get you under their control."

I shook my head incredulously.

"They could've just summoned me again. Why send the monsters?" I paused, contemplating my words. "They *did* send them, right?"

"Yeah, they did." Ronan sighed, sitting down on a rock in the field. "And apparently, they couldn't bring you back, but not for lack of trying. The conditions must be different this way around."

Shuddering, I thought of my accident before. Yeah, I had an inkling of what those conditions might have been.

"Long story short," Phillip took over, "we came to get you. We need to put an end to them once and for all."

I didn't get a chance to respond. Sirens were blaring through the night, and the red and blue lights of ambulances and police flashed in the distance, coming ever closer.

Not only that, but I heard a voice nearby.

"Ben?"

Vivienne.

I cursed under my breath. This was ... complicated.

"Ben, are you there?"

"Over here!" I shouted back.

I heard her scurrying through the grass toward us. As soon as she reached us, she clutched onto my arm, quickly surveying me for any injuries.

I rubbed her arm to reassure her that I was okay before gesturing at the rest of the group.

"Vivi, these are my friends from Halastaesia," I said. "Prince Phillip, Ronan, and Tara. Guys, this is Vivienne."

And so my two girlfriends from different worlds met.

Vivienne's eyes stuck to Tara, and I could feel her grip on my arm tighten. Yup. I didn't like this situation either. It made things too complicated. I hated complicated. The approaching sirens were a far cry from making things any easier for me.

"We should go. Like, now," I said, pointing back to the carnival.

We headed toward the car park without crossing through the carnival grounds, but the street had been blocked off by police vehicles, and the corresponding officers were questioning people exiting the carnival.

I gritted my teeth, trying to figure out how to get around this issue. I *really* didn't want to talk to police about my involvement in tonight's incident.

"Ben!"

Great. More people who I'd have to explain stuff to.

Jack's serious expression very clearly said that we needed to talk as he and David came jogging up to us. Now if Harvey were to appear as well, then everyone I might need to bring up to speed would be in one place, though the ideal place to do so was probably anywhere but here.

"Later, I promise," I told Jack, boring my gaze into his. He'd understand. He always did. Quietly, he nodded, and I sighed in relief. "We gotta get out of here first, but I don't think I want to be seen."

I pointed at my T-shirt covered in monster blood. Yeah. Fighting was messy business, and I had a feeling that with me like this, the police would have a field day questioning me.

"I can get us out," Tara promised. "You just need to tell me where to."

"Where to?" I echoed, but all I could think of was that I couldn't go home like this.

Jack glanced at Tara for a moment, and I could see his brain working. Did he connect my descriptions of her with the person standing in front of him? I had no clue.

"My place," he said eventually. "My mom is away for the night. We'll take the car."

"You go ahead. We'll meet you there," I promised, before turning to Vivienne. "You should go with him. He can take you home. I'm sorry about this, Vivi."

I gave her an apologetic grimace, but she shook her head. "It's alright."

Together they left, and I remained behind with my Halastaesian friends.

Tara did a quick chant, and a semi-transparent bluish sphere appeared around us. I was familiar with the spell — it made us practically invisible. The next spell she cast was a flying spell on the orb around us, and we lifted gently off the ground.

"Which way?" she asked.

I directed her, and we managed to land in Jack's garden before he'd made it home. He should be a while yet, since I wagered that they would be questioned by the police on their way, and then David would be taking Jack and Vivienne home.

That gave me some time to talk to my Halastaesian friends.

"How did you manage to come here, anyway?" I asked. "It's not exactly as easy as riding a horse to the next town."

Ronan sighed. "We performed a ritual. We've been collecting the ingredients for weeks ever since the summoning failed. We tried to bring you over, but it was difficult. It didn't help that when we were getting close, the mages and Corrupted Ones attacked in the middle of the ritual. So we did another one to come to you instead."

I thought of my nightmare that morning. That had been a few weeks ago for them? Halastaesia really did run faster than Earth, even now. No wonder Ronan and Phillip seemed older.

"I'm guessing that to go back to Halastaesia, we'd need to perform a similar ritual, huh?"

They nodded. They'd needed a few weeks to collect everything over there, I didn't even want to think about what those ingredients were.

"What's needed for it?"

Phillip pulled out a little pouch.

"We have most of it, in particular the things we knew would be used up in our ritual. Thing we knew from your stories we wouldn't be able to find here, like the ashes of a dragon's breath and stuff. But," he grimaced, "we thought that the ritual circle, including the items completing it, would travel with us, but they didn't."

"And what's that?"

Tara brushed her hair out of her face in one fluid motion. "We need a topaz still, and a bowl made from a hundred-year-old cedar tree."

Great. The topaz wouldn't be a problem, but the bowl might be tricky. I didn't exactly fancy felling a giant cedar myself just to carve out a tiny bowl, but depending on the circumstances, we might not have a choice.

"What about letting us be dragged back by the Corrupted Ones?" I asked, though I already had a bad feeling about it.

"I wouldn't recommend it," Tara said. "They'll only bring you straight to the silver-banded mages, and then everything will have been in vain."

"Now that they've discovered a way into your world, they won't settle with just Halastaesia, either," Ronan added. "Both worlds are in danger now."

I didn't really need the reminder. Obviously, I didn't want to see Halastaesia go down in ashes either. But apparently, I hadn't done as good a job saving it as I had believed. The realization made my chest feel heavy. This whole time, I'd genuinely believed I was a hero, that I'd saved a foreign realm from devastation and no longer had anything left for me, but in reality, I'd failed. Only half finished my mission. New determination filled me as anger replaced sadness. I would see it through to the end and save the world. Both of them.

The sound of gravel crunching under wheels in the driveway made me peek out over the garden gate. Vivienne was pulling in with Jack on the passenger seat. Apparently, she wanted explanations just as much as he did. Well … there was no way of hiding it from them. I'd just have to let them in on this whole mess. At least no one would think of me as the crazy one. Though, after everything that had happened this evening, I doubted that anyone could deny the truth. Near the end, too many people had seen the Corrupted Ones. There were too many signs of the devastation they'd laid down. No one could cover this up.

CHAPTER 15

Before long, we were facing each other across Jack's living room table.

After a moment of silence, Jack got right down to business.

"So it was all real then. The stories from your coma."

I nodded.

Jack looked from one of the Halastaesians to the next, correctly identifying each one of them.

"Then that would make you Tara, Phillip, and Ronan, huh?"

Ronan smirked. "And you must be Jack, the one who's been beating Ben in hand-to-hand combat since you met."

Jack chuckled. "Not anymore, not really." He glanced at me, and I couldn't help but be surprised. He was taking this revelation remarkably well. "I think I owe you an apology, bud."

I shook my head. "After the way you helped me deal with the Corrupted One, you don't owe me anything."

"Yeah, about that ..." He leaned forward in his

chair. "What the hell, dude? Why are all of your monsters showing up here? And, no offense, but why are *you* guys here?" The last part was directed at the Halastaesians.

"We're here to take this moron back to our world." Phillip jerked his thumb at me. "So that your world can go back to its safe tranquility, and he can *actually* save ours this time. As much as it pains me to say, he is the Chosen Hero after all." He rolled his eyes.

Oh, Phillip. Ever the ray of sunshine, aren't you? Still, his words stung a little. They were just a little too real for comfort.

He scoffed. "Some hero he is."

I didn't say anything. I didn't have anything to defend myself. Phillip was right. But someone else came to my defense instead.

"He *is* a hero!" Vivienne had stood up so abruptly, that her chair fell over backward. All eyes turned to her, mine more surprised than anyone else's. I'd never seen her so furious before—her eyes were practically aflame with anger. Her fists were clenched, and her jaw jutted forward as she repeated her words, more quietly, but no less firm.

"He *is* a hero. No hero can always succeed. But Ben always does everything he can, for everyone. It doesn't matter whether he even knows them, he just always does what's right. No matter what, he's always reliable, and he goes out of his way to help strangers. So how *dare* you imply that he's not a hero?"

Silence followed her outburst.

Then Tara smiled, crossed over to Vivienne, and pulled her a hug. "I couldn't agree more."

Meanwhile, I was still gaping at her. Where had *that* come from? I'd had no idea that she'd had such a high opinion of me—I mean, she'd had a crush on me for a little while, but I didn't know that this was how she saw me. I was a little stunned, wondering how I could possibly live up to such a miraculous image.

"But he'll still have to come with us. We need him. Our entire world needs him. And so does yours, now." Tara's gentle words hit home, both for Vivienne and I.

"Last time he went to your world he almost died, did you know that?" Jack's eyes had darkened. There was a defensiveness in his manners that I hadn't expected from him. "I sincerely hope you're not suggesting he do that again, because that ain't happening. Not again."

He had a point. I didn't really like the idea of almost dying again either. Especially considering how much grief I had caused everyone the previous time.

"Don't you worry." Ronan grinned. "We've got a ritual. He'll be just fine."

Somehow, I was starting to feel like a child caught between two parents arguing over custody. I cleared my throat to clink myself back into the conversation. "If we *can* manage to get back to Halastaesia, I'll go, even just to put all of this to rest. It's my fault for not finishing the job in the first place. But we have to get our hands on the missing ingredients first, and that might take a little time."

"Leave it to us. We'll take care of it." Phillip had dropped his haughty expression and stated it like a fact.

I nodded and turned to my Mitchell's Creek friends, who were both staring at me.

"You're actually going? You're leaving?" Vivienne looked like she was close to tears.

I could tell how much she was forcing herself not to glance at Tara. I would need to have a talk with her in private later. With both of them, actually. Separately. I needed to figure this situation out for myself before I could deal with this properly.

Jack was staring at me, too, though his glare expressed fierce determination. After a moment, he averted his scowl to the Halastaesians. "I'm coming, too."

Phillip only raised an eyebrow.

"Jack, I don't know if—"

"I'm going, whether you like it or not," he interrupted me, turning his glare back on me.

Welp, when he had his mind made up like that, there was no way to force him to change it. At most I could try to leave without him when the time came, though I was sure I would be paying for that bitterly afterward. He'd make sure of that.

"Me too." Vivienne's tears had given way to a determined gaze of her own, though hers was much more positive, and yet desperate at the same time. A lot less angry was the right way to put it.

It was Tara who interjected this time. "It's Vivienne, right?" Vivienne nodded so Tara continued, with a small, empathetic smile. "Coming along would be incredibly dangerous. Both Ben and Jack have combat training of some sort, and even with that it'll be tough. I can't let you put yourself in danger, not without a way to keep yourself safe. None of us would be able to protect you."

Vivienne scoffed. "Who said I need protecting?"

She pulled out her phone and opened her photos and videos app, pulling up a clip from one of her cheer offs. She pushed it in Tara's face.

"Does *this* look like I'm just some weak little girl that needs protecting?" She pushed her hip out, placing one hand on it with a confident smile. "I'm a cheerleader. Strong, flexible, and fast. So I don't have combat training. Big whoop. I'm smart. And you better believe that my kick would hurt like hell."

Tara watched the whole video. If she was surprised or confused by what she was watching—or by the phone—she didn't show it.

When the clip finished, she handed it back to Vivienne. "Point taken. I certainly don't want to fight you."

She was being nice. I had seen Tara fight often enough. No matter how impressive Vivienne's acrobatics were, Tara could beat her blindfolded. After all, she had all the grace and strength of a fae, not to mention magic. Even though I had to admit that Vivienne wasn't defenseless, I still didn't want her on this mission. I'd just have to employ the same strategy as with Jack—leave without telling either of them. It wasn't like they could make their own way.

The girls sat down again, both pacified.

I turned to Ronan. "Do you think the mages will attack again soon? How long would it normally take them to recharge their energy?"

I knew a little of how their society worked. They used different magic to someone like Tara, or to my own. It was overall more powerful but required a lot more preparation and time to recharge, but I had no idea how much energy their stunt earlier tonight would have cost them.

Ronan scratched his head. "I'm not sure. I think we'd normally have about a month or two."

My face fell when I recalculated that into our timeline.

"That only gives us a few days in this world," I told him, gritting my teeth. "Time works differently here."

No matter what, I didn't want to see a repeat of this evening. I didn't want to risk more people getting hurt.

We were on a deadline.

Phillip looked at me grimly. "Then we better get working."

Jack had been kind enough to let the Halastaesians stay with him overnight. I was grateful for it, because I really wasn't sure how to explain them to my mom. Vivienne drove me home, around four a.m. Just before I left the car to head inside, she stopped me with a gentle touch on my arm.

"Ben, this is all … insane."

"I know."

"But … I still believe in you." She looked at me, her eyes wide, as if asking for reassurance. She was pale, too.

We were all tired, and she'd gone through a lot today. A lot of scary experiences and emotional turmoil. And it wasn't about to stop only because she went home. It was doubtful that she'd get even a wink of sleep.

If I hadn't been completely exhausted, I wasn't sure that I would either.

I hugged her tightly and kissed her forehead.

"It'll be okay," I promised, though I knew I

was in no position to make a promise like that. Then again, I was the Chosen Hero, wasn't I? If I didn't fix everything, then what good was I?

She nodded and leaned into the hug.

"Ben, about Tara ..."

I froze, dreading her next words, though she hesitated to say them out loud. I didn't have an answer for her yet. All I knew was that I cared about them both. And come on, I'd loved Tara before I was torn from her so forcefully. And I continued to love her until I thought she wasn't real. But I loved Vivienne now, too—the girl who liked me despite all my vulnerabilities, who stood by me and supported me when I was more than a little damaged.

"Never mind."

She wasn't ready yet to find out. I felt relieved—more so than I had any right to be, and I resolved to talk to Tara tomorrow, to at least figure out for myself how I wanted to proceed. It was more than just a choice of which one of the girls I liked more. It was about which world I would choose after this was all over. I couldn't go traveling between them forever. I didn't even know if that'd be possible. So I had to pick one world. And along with it, one girl. But out of fairness to them both, I had to do it sooner rather than later.

For now though my first priority should still be to defeat our enemies.

I squeezed Vivienne tightly, before finally

getting out. "See you soon. Sleep tight."

"You too."

Her car remained motionless for a few minutes after I'd gotten out, and even when I closed the front door, I could see her still sitting in the car, looking forlorn.

A light was on in the living room. On tiptoes, holding my sword ready, I approached and peeked around the corner. But no monsters or mages waited for me there. Just Mom, huddled in a blanket, staring at the phone, as if willing it to ring.

"Mom?" I leaned the sword against the doorway so she wouldn't see it and entered. "Are you okay?"

Clearly she hadn't heard me opening the door, because her fearful gaze shot up to me and changed to complete and utter relief.

Throwing the blanket aside and knocking over a coffee mug in the process, she jumped up and raced over, embracing me tightly.

"Where have you been?" she asked. "I was so worried! Harvey's mom called—she had to pick him up from the hospital! And there were other people from the carnival there and … What in the world happened?"

She held me at arm's length, looking me up and down as if to reassure herself I had no injuries. Boy was I glad I'd borrowed some of Jack's clothes before I'd come home. I would not have enjoyed explaining the blood to her.

"I'm fine, Mom."

I hugged her to reassure her, but I could feel her trembling in my arms. I could only imagine how scared she must have been. I'd lost my phone at the carnival somewhere while fighting, but I could guess that I probably had close to a hundred missed calls from her.

"What happened?" she repeated.

What could I possibly tell her?

"I don't really know what happened at the carnival, but Jack, Vivi, and I left early. We were at his house hanging out and kind of lost track of time. Is Harvey okay?"

I considered it a white lie. It would save her from further worrying and save me from having to explain that my hallucinations were real and that Dr. Steinberg was oh so wrong.

She nodded absent-mindedly, slowly calming.

"He had a few scratches. Apparently, there was some kind of panic at the carnival. Stacey said something about a terrorist attack ..."

How typical of Harvey's family to jump to the most dramatic yet somewhat realistic thing they could come up with. I didn't even want to know what he'd suggest on Monday. Or else, what he'd ask me. Though how he might still deny my experience, I didn't know.

"Really?" I widened my eyes, trying to play up the shock. "Gosh, that's awful! I hope no one was seriously injured! Did they get whoever caused it?"

She shook her head.

"I really don't know … I'm just so relieved you're okay!"

She hugged me again and then yawned.

"Now, off to bed with both of us."

I was so tired, I wouldn't have dreamed of arguing.

CHAPTER 16

First thing the next morning, I cycled over to Jack's house, ready to help in the search for the ritual items.

I found the Halastaesians in the middle of breakfast, Jack astonishing everyone with all the different Earth varieties and choices. He made a big show of it all for them, and even went so far as to make omelets.

When I arrived, he just included me in the mix.

"Ben," Tara said, holding up her slice of bread. "Look, have you tried this pee-nut-butter thing? It's so good!" She twisted her eyes to show how much she loved it, before digging into it again with gusto.

I smirked. "I've tried it all right."

While I loved Halastaesia, I couldn't claim that it had a lot of variety in terms of food. It was all the same kind of magical adventure gruel you'd expect, really. It made me wonder if my world seemed as magical and wondrous to them as theirs had to me.

"Okay, battle plan," I said when it seemed like everyone had had their fill of breakfast. "I think we should split up."

Jack nodded in agreement. "I can scour the internet for info."

"The internet?" Ronan's eyes lit up.

Ah yes. Of course I'd told them of the internet way back when. He'd always been fascinated by the idea of it. After all, it was a resource of unlimited knowledge and an easy way for anyone to acquire almost anything. It meant that luxuries were no longer confined to the rich and powerful, although, living in a capitalist world, they could certainly get their fill more easily.

"You wanna watch?" Jack asked, raising an eyebrow.

Ronan grinned. "You bet'cha."

That left Phillip, Tara, and me.

"We can check out the mall, see what we can find there."

The internet was definitely a more likely place to succeed, but if we needed to put in a custom order or have something delivered from far away, it might cost us precious time. Besides, sometimes it was easier to find something special in a small, independent store somewhere.

While Phillip muttered in awe about horseless carriages below us as Tara flew us to the mall, I laid out the plan for them.

"I've got some money, so just see if you can find the topaz or the bowl in a shop. You can ask around, but don't try to take anything out of the shops. Come find me first!"

Phillip rolled his eyes. "Obviously. We're not thieves, you know."

I glanced at him, remembering how his princely highness had liked to practice his hand at sleight of hand in the marketplace when I'd first met him. That kind of thing wouldn't go down well here. Not with all the alarms and camera set up. Still, he'd been warned.

"Don't draw too much attention to yourselves," I added and glanced down at them, grimacing. "If anyone asks about your clothing, tell them you're working on a period drama for school and you're on your break, or something. Or maybe a LARP."

They both nodded, albeit with some perplexed confusion on their faces, and we split.

Or so I thought.

Planning to go around the first few storefronts to see if the stores were likely to have anything of use in them, I had only made it to the first shop when the scent of primroses wafted over to me.

Tara was standing beside me, peering at the store's display.

"It's so good to see you," she said and took my hand, intertwining my fingers with her own. "I thought I'd never get to do that again."

"Me either," I admitted, and, holding hands, we strolled from store window to store window.

I was happy to see Tara again. It was comforting and nice to smell her natural scent and see how her dark eyes gently brushed over everything she saw, so casually, even though I knew she was taking in every detail. Walking beside her felt strange, after months of being apart from her, but nevertheless, it also felt familiar and comfortable.

But something was nagging at me. This felt different compared to when I walked like this with Vivienne. Not in a bad way, but not in a good way either. Just … different.

I tried to keep my attention on our goal, and we stopped in front of a jewelry store that seemed to have tons of pendants and earrings made from gemstones. Surely they'd have something made from topaz in there!

"Let's check it out."

The eager salesperson with an overly cheerful fake smile plastered on his face was already approaching us the second we stepped through the door. "May I help you?"

I wasn't overly surprised. This place looked like somewhere my parents might go. In other words, not somewhere a typical teenager could afford. I'd saved up some money from part-time jobs that I'd had before my accident, and it was a decent enough sum, but whether it would be enough for what we needed … Well, there was only one way to find out.

"Hi." I put on my most charming smile and theatrically placed my arm around Tara. "We're looking for something made with topaz. She just adores it, don't you, sweetie?" Playing up the lovey-dovey bit, I turned to her.

She joined in instantly, batting her eyelids coquettishly. "I do. It's just so pretty, don't you agree?"

The clerk's smile grew a little strained. "Yes, quite. Follow me, I believe I have just the thing."

He proceeded to show us a collection of earrings, necklaces, and bracelets that used topaz gems, but Tara inspected each and shook her head. While I didn't know why she declined them all, I was certain she had her reasons. As a fae, she was connected closer to anything natural than humans could imagine, and she could feel things we couldn't.

"I'm sorry," she eventually said, smiling apologetically at the clerk. "It doesn't seem like you have what I'm looking for. I hope you have a lovely day, though!"

The clerk's smile grew even more exasperated, but he managed to keep it together and wish us good luck.

I gave Tara a questioning glance, and she shrugged.

"None of them were pure enough. We need something more raw."

Raw, huh? The only shop I could think of that

might carry something like that was a small store on Main Street. Well, it was worth a shot.

"This way," I said, and we wove through the crowds. I didn't think I would need to tell Phillip where we were going. We wouldn't be long, and he was likely busy anyway, never mind that finding him in the mall would be a difficult task to begin with.

"Ben?"

"Oh. My. Gosh."

I cursed inwardly and took a deep breath before letting go of Tara's hand as I turned around to Harvey and Cindy.

He looked furious, and she looked plainly shocked.

My gaze went straight to his shoulder where he'd been injured, the bandages peeking out from under his sweatshirt. It didn't seem to bother him too much, at least.

"What the hell, dude? First you vanish last night, and now you're gallivanting off with some random chick?"

Huh. I hadn't expected him to instantly confront me about Tara.

"This is Tara," I said, hoping that he'd understand, combining last night's events and hearing her name. After all, he'd seen a Corrupted One firsthand.

He looked like he wanted to spit in my face.

"I couldn't care less what her name is. I just really didn't expect this from you, of all people."

Disgusted, he turned away. My gut twisted to see him think so little of me. I knew him well enough to realize that nothing I said right now would get through to him. I'd have to wait until he cooled off, apologize, and then make him listen to my explanation.

"Poor Vivi," Cindy whispered, still looking shocked by the new revelation.

"Listen, last night—"

"What about it?" He stared blankly back at me.

"The monsters ..." I didn't know where to go from there.

"What monsters?"

I froze. I knew for a fact he'd seen a Corrupted One. It had injured him—his arm still had a bandage on it.

"What happened at the carnival—" I began anew, but he interrupted me.

"The gas leak? Yeah. Made a lot of people go crazy." His eyes flashed to Tara, and he glared at me. "But don't you dare use that as an excuse. Vivi deserves better than that."

They walked off, leaving us standing. I felt awful. Downright gutted.

I couldn't even dream of making him understand the difficult position I was in, with him thinking that a gas leak had caused all the previous night's events, potentially even mass hallucinations the way these stories went. There was no possible way he would ever believe me now. I'd just lost one of my best friends.

He was right, too, at least as far as Vivienne was concerned. She did deserve better. In that moment, I determined that I *would* do better. I loved her. And as much as I loved Halastaesia and Tara, I had made my choice.

Tara and I were looking through the small esoteric store, looking at healing rocks and rock gemstones along with carved wooden bowls of every size.

"Vivienne and you … You're close, aren't you?" she asked, after we'd been looking around in silence for a while.

Great. Now I had to have this conversation, too. I dreaded having to hurt her, but I didn't see a way around it, not now that I had made my decision to stay with Vivienne.

I nodded.

"After I was sent back here … home, I started thinking that it might all have been a dream," I admitted. "Halastaesia, the Corrupted Ones, you."

Sighing, she ran her fingers through her long, black hair. "I can see how that would happen in a world like this. There doesn't seem to be a lot of space for magic here. Not even in a place like this."

She gestured at the store around us—a store

literally dedicated to mystic arts and witchcraft. I chuckled. The Wiccans wouldn't be happy to hear that.

She grew silent again for a moment, before meeting my eyes.

"A lot of time has passed. And a lot of things have changed."

She bit her lip, as if trying to determine how to put her words. She was struggling with something, that much was clear. She turned her head away from me, ashamed.

"I've been feeling so guilty for months ... But I just ... Ronan ..."

It was rare to see a young woman normally so strong and confident, weak and vulnerable. But I understood what she was telling me. I'd always thought that if I hadn't come along, she and Ronan would eventually find to each other.

I smiled at her, relieved that I had already made my own choice and that it would cause her no pain.

"No need to feel guilty anymore. Maybe in the grand scheme of things, we just weren't meant to be. I still care about you. A lot. And I know you do, too. But I think that maybe this is for the best."

She smiled, though her eyes were watery. I knew how she felt. I felt the same sense of loss, the same unwillingness to let go of what we'd had in the past. It had been special. But now I was starting to think it was special because of the adventure we'd been on. *I* was special because I was the Chosen Hero—a mysterious boy from another world. *She* was special because she was a beautiful fae—a magical creature who also happened to be the first girl to ever pay attention to me. Add that to the adventure as a whole, and you basically had yourself a typical fantasy novel.

"Probably ..." She grew quiet as her gaze glided across the merchandise in front of her—all sorts of knickknacks and witchcraft paraphernalia.

Frankly, I was surprised the store didn't also sell pointy black hats. They already carried the matching cloaks and capes in the back.

"Hey, look at this!" She picked up a bowl that was holding a lot of small rocks. It looked older than the kind of stuff they sold to you nowadays, more run down. The pattern on the wood was pretty and dark.

"It's cedar," she said, running a finger along the outside. "But how old?"

We turned to the salesclerk who sat at her desk, and I caught a glimpse of her computer screen. It looked like she was doing an online quiz to find out which color her aura was. I didn't even want to know how often she'd done that one hoping for different results.

"Excuse me," Tara said, crossing over to her. "Could you tell me how old the tree was when it was cut to make this bowl?"

There was no way the clerk would know something like that. Not for this.

She stared at Tara, blinking slowly as her brain caught up to her ears.

"The tree ..." she repeated, looking down at the bowl with a concentrated expression. She picked it up and lifted it up to see the markings. Her lips moved as she counted the lines, and I had to keep from groaning. I should have expected this.

She set the bowl down again.

"About twenty years, at least," she said confidently. "Maybe more. But this bowl is an antique, it's not really for sale, you know."

Tara was about to reply, but I shook my head softly. Instead of the sharp reply sitting ready on her tongue, she forced herself to smile and thank the clerk. We wouldn't find anything useful here after all. I doubted the tree for that bowl had been old enough anyway. Once we had left the store, Tara sighed deeply.

"So disheartening!"

I shrugged but I didn't disagree. We'd just have to see if Phillip or the other team had been in more luck.

Phillip had found not only a figurine of a bird made from topaz, he'd also found a woodworking shop just outside of the mall, on the edge of the industrial quarter. We went to check out both, but the figurine wasn't pure enough, according to Tara, and the woodwork master couldn't help us out either. While he did work with cedar, his trees were usually younger than what we needed.

"I can keep an eye out for an older one though. Why so specific, anyway?"

Before either of the other two could answer with the truth, I jumped in.

"It's for a research project. We compare the patterns of decorative items crafted from the same wood but made from different ages in a tree. We've got the younger ones, but those older ones are hard to come by."

I shrugged, hoping that my excuse wasn't too lame. He did look perplexed, but then he shrugged.

"Weird projects they give you kids in school these days, huh? Oh well. Good luck with it anyway. Do you want to leave a number for me to call if I find something?"

I scribbled down my cell phone number on the piece of paper he held out to me, and then we left.

I sighed. We had been spectacularly unsuccessful.

"Back to base?" I asked the other two.

They nodded, not looking nearly as disheartened as I was feeling. They came from a

world where things often took a little longer and
you didn't have the convenience of a shopping
mall on your doorstep. The problem was that,
starting tomorrow, I was going to be limited in
my movement. Not only did I have to go to
school, I also had my appointment with Dr.
Steinberg, and I couldn't miss either one without
Mom being alerted right away. Since I was going
to disappear soon for a while when I returned to
Halastaesia, I didn't want to risk doing anything
that would worry her unnecessarily before that
time came. With time passing differently, I was
hoping that I could resolve everything there and
come back without even taking a whole day.

By the time we got back to Jack's place, I was
feeling thoroughly guilty on all fronts. I couldn't
see any way forward that would make everyone
happy without causing grief.

"Anything?" I asked as we stumbled through
the door.

Jack shrugged and guided me through a few
tabs on his browser. He'd uncovered some
vendors who sold raw topaz, still partially
enclosed in rock.

I turned to Tara. "Would something like that
be pure enough?"

Her brows knit together as she leaned in to

look at it more closely. "It's difficult to say without having it in front of me, but ... I think so. If it's anything like the natural topaz from Halastaesia, at least."

I glanced at the price. It would be costly, but I thought I could just about cover it with some of the money I'd saved up.

"Let's try it."

No sooner had we ordered the topaz for delivery, than the doorbell rang.

Phillip's eyes sparkled in surprise. "I know you said that the postal service in your world was fast, but this is incredible!"

He raced to the door before I could reply and opened it. I ran after him, trying to prevent any potential disaster from happening. No matter how express the delivery service was, even they hadn't learned how to teleport.

The person waiting outside was Vivienne.

Guilt made my heart drop into my stomach when her eyes landed on me and disappointment washed over them. I couldn't blame her for feeling betrayed. I intentionally hadn't told her I was coming here today. I didn't want her to get involved more than she'd needed to. But instead, I'd spent the day with Tara. And while I knew the decision I'd made, and how we stood to each other, Vivienne didn't. And I wouldn't be surprised if ...

"Cindy called me."

Yep. Saw that one coming.

Her voice was trying too hard to be emotionless; she was putting too much effort into seeming dispassionate and aloof. It only served to make me feel worse.

I had nothing to say.

"When she mentioned that she saw you with Tara, I knew you guys were working away without me." She flapped her arms to her sides. "So I came."

Phillip had tactfully retreated, leaving the two of us in the doorway alone.

She gave me a small smile, though the pain in the corners of her eyes wasn't something she could hide. I needed to talk to her. Make things right.

I glanced back at the others, who were all suspiciously intently hanging over Jack's small notebook laptop. They could manage without me for a little while.

"Let's go for a walk," I said, and closed the door after stepping outside.

She followed me quietly, half a step behind me. I wanted to tell her about Tara and I, but I didn't know how to start. I played out different phrases and terminologies in my head, trying to predict how she might react to different ones, but in the end, I still couldn't settle on anything.

We walked all the way down to the river, and then along its banks.

In the end, I awkwardly pointed at a bench. "Wanna sit?"

She shook her head, but still avoided eye contact. It occurred to me that she was looking paler than normal.

"Why do you not want me to help?" she asked, as if she was expecting to hear the answer she was already thinking in her head.

I watched her for a moment, contemplating how fragile she seemed, and yet how much strength she'd shown just yesterday.

"Vivi …" I stepped closer to her. "You're the person I care for the most. I couldn't take it if something happened to you."

She didn't react, and I closed the distance between us, pulling her close to me. After a moment, her hands grasped my T-shirt, and she clung to it tightly. Time to put all her worries to rest.

"You don't need to worry about Tara either," I added. "It's you I love and want to be with, okay?"

Her face was buried against my chest, but I could feel her nod.

"So I want you to stay out of this. And I promise that when all of this is over, I'll come back to you."

Now she pulled herself from my grasp and glared up at me, though her eyes were swimming.

"Don't you dare," she snapped. "I'm coming. I don't care what you say, I'm not letting you go without me."

Seeing her stand there defiantly, angry in her protectiveness, I couldn't help but think how she really did look strong. Her emotions gave her strength, and I wanted to believe that she would be fine, that she really could fight beside me. Before I knew what in the world I was doing, I had nodded.

A confident smile crossed her face.

"That's better." She wiped her last tears away and fixed her hair before she gave me another challenging smile and raised one eyebrow. "What are you waiting for? Let's go back. We have work to do, don't we?"

CHAPTER 17

The weekend's activities had clearly taken more out of me than I'd realized, because I overslept the next morning. On my cycle to school, I went over what I should tell Dr. Steinberg. Obviously, I couldn't tell her the full truth, so I had to mix up a convincing lie.

I'd stopped taking the medication, since it had turned out that my "hallucinations" hadn't been illusions after all. More than ever, I needed my head to be clear. Really clear. I didn't want to risk not seeing a Corrupted One materialize in front of me because some pills were messing with my perception.

My eyes were drawn to every dark shadow I passed. When I was waiting at a traffic light, I was expecting a Corrupted One to rise from the ground in front of me. When I cycled uninterrupted down a straight path, I felt as if something was behind me, chasing after me. In short, my nerves were on the edge the entire way to school, my body tense. How long would it take for the silver-banded mages to get their act together and come back for me?

I received my late note and sat in the back of my algebra class. Harvey didn't even so much as look at me. I wondered if I'd get a chance to talk to him about Saturday. I wanted to. If only to give him an explanation of what had happened, and to prove to him that everything I'd told him was the truth.

Harvey dashed my hopes the second the bell rang by pulling a disappearing act. I missed my chance.

I was betting on getting a second chance by lunch time, but I couldn't bring myself to enter the cafeteria. As I stood in the entrance, I stared at the masses of people in front of me, and all my senses went into overdrive trying to take everything in at once.

In the end, I gave up and ate outside. At the very least no one would be able to sneak up on me.

Vivienne found and joined me before long.

"I saw you leave the cafeteria," she said by ways of explanation. "What's up? You okay?"

I nodded and gave her a half smile. "Just too many people in there right now. I wouldn't be able to relax."

After a moment's hesitation, she pulled up the app of the local newspaper on her phone. "Have you seen this?" She pointed at the top article.

Monsters invade carnival!

It was clickbait. While I hadn't seen this exact article, I'd seen others like it. The official story to explain the Corrupted Ones away was that there'd been a natural gas leak that had caused mass hallucinations. Now, the entire area around the carnival was off limits for anyone except the experts who were investigating and containing said "gas leak". All the injuries were reported to have occurred as a result of the ensuing panic. It wasn't a bad explanation as far as these things went, and it would explain why not everyone had noticed the monsters. It also got me off the hook if anyone should recognize me.

"It's incredible. I was talking to the others and it's like it never happened. None of them even want to admit to seeing those ... those creatures, never mind even considering for an instant that it was real."

She shook her head in disbelief, but I could only shrug. I had some experience in distrusting my own senses because of the world telling me that what I saw couldn't possibly be real.

"It's better than if people started panicking for real. Or, imagine if this became a bigger thing. I guarantee you we'd start getting theories about how Russia is trying to invade with some kind of new bioengineered superweapon." I rolled my eyes.

Vivienne sighed and clicked through to another page of the paper, pointing to a short article.

"Already there, I'm afraid. They're saying

either Russia or China."

Why was it that people were so predictable?

We sat beside each other, eating for a few moments in silence. Then Vivienne spoke up again.

"Cindy and Harvey are still mad at you," she said, avoiding looking at me. "They didn't believe me when I said that everything was alright. They said I was blinded by love."

She sighed and glanced up at me coquettishly. "Am I?"

Grinning, I put my arms around her. "Of course not."

I placed a kiss on her temple, and she giggled.

"That's what I thought. So what are we doing now? Are we just going to wait for the stone to arrive and hope that your woodworking contact will be able to get his hands on a cedar that's old enough?"

"More or less, yeah. Though Jack's calling up more woodworkers in the state today, and the others are going through the woods to see if they can find a tree that would work."

"You're just gonna cut it down?"

She seemed so shocked at the notion, it immediately made me feel guilty.

"Not unless we have to," I was quick to assert. "It's just a precaution. We don't want to wait until the Corrupted Ones come back, and we may not be able to get our hands on the bowl any other way. But we might always be able to just cut a thick branch. I don't know how big the bowl has to be, but I'm certain Tara would never harm a plant more than she absolutely needed to."

Vivienne leaned back and looked up at the sky, a mystified expression on her face. "So she's really a fae, huh?"

"A flower fae. Primroses are her mark," I specified.

Stretching, she sighed. "I am so glad I don't have to compete with her."

She sure was bringing this up a lot. I'd thought that once I told her that I wanted to be with her, everything would be fine and go back to normal between us, but this whole Tara issue was clearly occupying her mind a whole lot more than I'd realized. I had no idea how to put her at ease, if that was even possible.

"Are you going back to Jack's after school?" she asked then, standing up.

"No, I have to go see my shrink."

"Really?" She seemed mystified by my response. "Even though you know it was real now?"

I shrugged. "If I don't, my mom will worry. And especially after this weekend, I kinda need to, though I'll be telling her total hogwash."

"Are you sure that's a good idea?"

No. Absolutely not.

"Sure," I said. "Besides, I don't think there's much left for me to do until we get the items we need. But tomorrow," I stood up next to her, "you, Jack, and I are going to do some training. If you two are going to join us, you'll need to know how to fight properly."

She placed her hand on her hip and popped it out with a confident smirk. "About time."

I tried to catch Harvey again after last period, but he completely blanked me when I walked up to him by the lockers and practically ran off. I was left with no option other than to prepare for my appointment with Dr. Steinberg, and to call up Jack while I was waiting in front of her office to find out how the search was going.

He gave a quick and simple answer.

Not well.

A rush of anxiety flushed through my body when I thought about how we were running out of time. How soon before the mages would make another attempt to get to me? I still didn't know exactly how I had stolen what they needed, or how I could possibly extract it to either give it to them, or to use it against them. Tara had said something about my *magic*, but it wasn't like I was able to use it the way I had in Halastaesia, so it must be something more phantasmal.

I didn't like this. I didn't like this at all. Plus, I

still saw Corrupted Ones lurking in every shadow at the edge of my vision, and that feeling only dissipated when I looked at it directly. It was like they were already waiting for me, holding out for some invisible signal to leave their hiding place and come for me. Only the rational part of my brain stopped me from freaking out completely.

They weren't really here. Not yet.

What I was seeing was my mind playing tricks on me, an illusion it conjured up in fear and anxiety. If nothing else, it kept me vigilant about surveying my surroundings.

"Hello, Ben." Dr. Steinberg had a strained smile on her face as she greeted me.

She looks pale today, I thought. As if she hadn't slept well.

"Hi," I said and sat down on the bench. "How are you today?"

"I'm doing well, thank you for asking."

Liar. I could see the rings under her eyes and the nervous twitching of her fingers.

"How about you? Shall we begin?"

"I'm doing alright, I guess. Had a fairly uneventful week with the exception of a nightmare on Friday," I lied as I lay down. Boy, my weekend couldn't possibly have been more eventful if I'd decided to climb Mount Everest on a whim.

"Oh, really?" Her voice had a barely noticeable nervous shake. She cleared her throat. "Why don't you tell me about your nightmare?"

So I told her. The fact that the nightmare had actually been my soul being briefly transported thanks to a ritual my friends performed I left out, but as far as nightmares went, it worked with the rest of the narrative she knew of so far.

"Could you describe the monsters and your friends in a little more detail?"

I'd brushed over the in-depth explanations since I'd already spoken about those early on, but her wanting to hear about them again made me perk up. Something told me that this session was no longer just for me.

I repositioned myself a little, so I could observe her from the corner of my vision and described the Corrupted Ones before I moved on to tell her about Tara, Ronan, and Phillip.

The shake in her hand grew stronger, and her breathing more rapid. That much I could tell even without looking. When I actually turned to meet her gaze after my explanation, she had taken on an almost deathly complexion and her lips were pressed into two thin lines.

"Doc," I said, hesitantly, "were you at the carnival on Saturday?"

"Oh," she laughed, overly cheerful. "You went too, didn't you? You were looking forward to it."

No mistaking it. She wanted me to talk about the carnival, and about the monsters. No doubt she'd expected me to burst into the office and start babbling about them right away. And her reaction must mean … she'd seen them. And considering her interest in the Halastaesians, there was a good chance she'd seen my friends fight and kill the Corrupted Ones.

So what now? Did I tell her the truth and hope she would believe it, or would I tell her the same story I'd told my mom, allowing her to make herself believe that it had just been a mass hallucination like the paper suggested? She was acting differently than Harvey, Rod, Cindy, and Lauren. She was still fighting with herself on what to believe.

"I was there." I looked straight at her, meeting her gaze evenly. "Doc, what did you see?"

I tried to be gentle in my tone, yet firm. She needed to say it, I could tell as much. Whatever was playing on her mind, she needed an outlet, and while I knew that most psychologists saw another psychologist to help with stuff like that, I figured in this scenario, it was me she needed to talk to.

"Oh, no, let's not talk about me," she warded me off. "We're here to talk about you, after all. Are you still taking your medication?"

I shook my head. No point in lying about this.

"How come?"

She seemed to already suspect the answer.

"There didn't seem to be a point in it anymore."

"And why is that?"

I didn't respond. Instead, I just watched her. She was holding her notepad and pen, like always. But her hands were trembling. She really wasn't in any state to provide therapy to anyone right now.

I sighed. "Doc, let's take a break from the session for a moment. Tell me what you saw. Please?"

She hesitated, desperately clinging to her professionalism.

"There was a gas leak at the carnival," she said, though her words sounded hollow to say the least. "I was concerned that it might have given you flashbacks to your coma dreams, since they created hallucinations in so many people."

I shook my head. "I didn't have any hallucinations." I watched her clench and unclench her shoulders. I had a feeling that she was more inclined to believe my previous tales of Halastaesia now. Maybe she'd even seen Tara do magic at the carnival. Perhaps she'd seen me fight. "And I'm going to make sure that no one else is going to see monsters like that ever again."

An inane statement at a first glance, but someone who had spent as much talking with me as Dr. Steinberg had over the past few months would understand my meaning. I had no reservations. She'd seen more than she'd thought possible, whatever that might have been exactly. It had changed her perception of the world in some shape or form and while she was struggling to come to terms with it right now, it could go either direction.

It was up to her what she wanted to believe.

"I should go," I said. "Maybe you should take a few days off some time soon, Doc. You look like you might need it."

I left without either one of us saying anything more. At the end of the day, she needed to come to terms with whatever reality she chose on her own. But I was relieved that not everyone decided to believe the newspaper story without reservations like Harvey did. I could imagine that I would continue to go see Dr. Steinberg after all of this was over. If only to deal with the aftermath. Settling back into normality wouldn't be easy, though I imagined that it wouldn't be as much of a problem as it had been before.

But first, I had a mission.

CHAPTER 18

"Anything?"

I had cycled over to Jack's place immediately to check in with him, since I had some time before Mom expected me home.

He only shook his head. "No idea if the others found something, though. They haven't come back yet."

I flopped down on the living room couch. "What's your mom saying about them being here, by the way?"

He shrugged. "I told her they're exchange students from Europe but the families where they were staying couldn't keep them for the moment because of what happened Saturday."

"And she bought that?"

Another shrug. "She likes having people around."

I wondered how she would deal with not having anyone suddenly, even if it was only for a short while. With Jack going to Halastaesia with us, she'd be left all alone, much like my own mom. Maybe there was something we could do for them, even just to stop them from noticing immediately.

The topaz should be arriving tomorrow. Now it was just a question of how soon we could get our hands on the bowl. But that wasn't the only thing on my mind.

"We've got to get Vivi and you in shape."

He raised one eyebrow and a confident smirk appeared on his face. "Want me to prove to you right now how in shape I am?"

I smirked right back. "You'll lose, but … you're on."

We went out in the garden to have more space and began sparring. Within seconds, he had to tap out.

"Again," he growled. "I wasn't ready that time."

I bit back the remark that an enemy wouldn't wait for him to get ready, and helped him up instead. This time, I waited for him to attack. I evaded him effortlessly with a single sidestep, grabbing his arm and pulling it into a hold with ease. I added the tiniest amount of pressure to show him how simple it would be to break it from this position, but he didn't give in. Instead, he rolled out of the lock, pulling his arm from my grasp in the process, and went for a kick to the side of my leg. Again, I stepped out of the way, pivoting on the other foot, and went for a kick myself to swipe the arm he was leaning on. The moment he lost his balance, I dropped my knee on his throat, pinning both his arms down with my legs.

He tapped out.

"You're way too fast," he gasped. "You were holding back before."

I nodded. No point in false modesty right now.

"Your movements get hectic and uncoordinated the moment I speed up past your comfort zone," I told him as I helped him up. "And *that's* why we need to get you in shape."

"Alright, I get it."

"It was a good start, though." Tara materialized in the garden, one hand on the shoulders of our other friends.

Damn, I hadn't even noticed them. I was usually good at sensing her presence, even when she was cloaking herself. She must have trained a lot since my time in Halastaesia.

"When did you get here?" I asked.

Phillip shrugged. "Early enough to watch that pitiful display. You really need to get back to training. It's painfully obvious that you've been slacking off."

His words were directed at me, not Jack. The worst part was that I couldn't even deny it. He was absolutely right. I wasn't in as good shape as I had been in Halastaesia, not by a long shot. But that made me worry even more about Vivienne and Jack who couldn't even hold a candle to me in my current state.

"I've got this." Ronan grinned, patting Phillip's shoulder jovially. His eyes were gleaming far more than I liked. He was plotting and scheming, and with Ronan, that was never a good sign.

"But first," Tara gave him a warning glance, the kind I knew far too well, "we found a tree that should work. It's pretty far, but it's also quite large. We should be able to cut a branch large enough."

"Awesome! Have you made the bowl with your hocus pocus yet?" Jack asked, but she shook her head.

"It doesn't work like that. Well, I could, but it wouldn't work for what we need. It has to be carved by hand, or at least by simple tools. Magic would taint it."

"So I'm guessing you need tools to cut it as well, huh?" I asked.

She nodded just as my phone buzzed in my pocket. I fished it out quickly in case it was a text message from Vivienne or Mom, but instead, I saw a number unknown to me. However, a quick scan over the message brightened my expression immediately.

"Scratch that. Looks like the woodworker got his hands on what we need. He says we can pick it up on Thursday."

I shot him a quick response, thanking him and confirming that I was still interested in the bowl, adding a quick reference picture from the web for him as well.

"That's wonderful!"

I made a quick calculation in my head. At some point between now and Thursday, the topaz we'd ordered should arrive, which made Friday probably the best day to perform our ritual to travel to Halastaesia. If we only spent the weekend away, we should have about a week there before we needed to return. For the kind of sting mission we had in mind, that might be enough, but I had no idea if that was truly the case. Either way, the weekend opened up options to distract our mothers from our absence.

I turned to Jack. "How would you feel about giving our moms an all-expenses-paid spa weekend?"

I skipped school the next day, pretending to be my dad to call in sick. I still left the house at the same time as usual, but instead of my books and gym clothes, I carried my gym clothes in my bag and headed to Jack's place. His mom had already left for work, and he'd asked her to excuse him from school as well because he wasn't feeling great.

I'd texted Vivienne last night, telling her about the plan. She would never forgive me if I left her out of the loop now. And truthfully, I didn't want to anymore. I was still worried about her safety, but if Corrupted Ones could show up, I'd rather have her with me.

When Phillip let me into Jack's kitchen, Vivienne was already there, talking quietly with Tara. It looked like they might be starting to get along. If that was true, it'd be great. If nothing else, it would probably reassure Vivienne even more.

"I'm here and I'm ready." I dropped my bag and looked around. "Shall we get started?"

Tara rose gracefully to her feet.

"Phillip and I are going to scan the area and check for enemy movement. And you three," she looked between Vivienne, Jack, and me with a smirk, "are going to get beaten into shape."

"Hope you're ready," Ronan chimed in cheerfully, cracking his knuckles.

While I'd known this was coming, I still winced inwardly. Our tank was about to smash us into pieces. But better him than the Corrupted Ones.

"So how do we do this?" Jack flexed his fingers, a cocky grin already spreading across his face, despite his loss to me the other day. Poor guy. He had no idea what was waiting for him.

"First, I gotta see what I'm working with. Let's spar outside."

Ronan turned to the terrace door, but Jack held him back.

"We're actually all meant to be in school right

now, so why don't we stay inside? It'd be bad if someone saw us."

Ronan shrugged. "Inside works just as well. Just make sure there's nothing breakable around when we start."

Vivienne and Jack shared a glance before looking at me. I only shrugged. When Ronan got serious, things could get messy. I knew that better than anyone.

"Listen to him," I advised them. "He's a joker, but there are some things he doesn't kid around with."

As the three of them began clearing a space in the living room to spar, I stood aside with Phillip and Tara and handed them a map from the area along with binoculars I'd packed for them. "Here, I thought these might come in handy."

"Thanks, Ben. That should be a great help! We're off then," Tara said, and placed her hand on Phillips shoulder, before they vanished.

It was late afternoon when Ronan decided he had sufficiently pummeled us.

Jack, Vivienne, and I were lying sprawled across the living room furniture, desperately trying to catch our breaths and ignore the pain from our injuries. Sure, they were mostly small bruises and stretched ligaments, and Tara could heal them in a flash whenever she'd be back, but they still hurt. As expected, I'd fared better than Jack, who was probably reconsidering all of his life choices right about now. But Vivienne had come as a surprise to everyone. I'd never realized how much strength and speed it took to be a cheerleader, but I was starting to reconsider my previous stance. With her agility and leg strength, I wasn't certain that I could win in a hand-to-hand match against her. She'd even given Ronan a good run for his money.

I made a mental note never to underestimate a girl again. Where Jack had shown hesitation to strike, perhaps because of his training, Vivienne had shown none. She wasn't above using dirty tricks either. Man, girls were scary.

I shuddered.

"Not bad for a start." Ronan smirked, watching us all pity ourselves. "It's something we can build on at least. Which is good, considering how little time we have."

He was sounding far too cheerful about this situation.

The doorbell rang, cutting off whatever snarky reply I was holding back. I glanced at Jack, but he didn't seem to be in any position to move to answer the door, and I wasn't sure that I wanted Ronan to be the one doing the talking. After all, this world was still unfamiliar to him, after all.

So I grunted as I pulled myself to my feet and snatched the dressing gown Jack had brought for disguise's sake, before shuffling to the door, ensuring to look miserable. It wasn't difficult.

A delivery person was waiting out front, pen and paper ready in hand to get my signature.

"Sorry for the delay," I said nasally. "I just woke up."

Hoping he'd buy my staying-home-from-school-because-I'm-sick act, I took the pen and signed for the package.

"Hope you feel better, son," he said as he tipped his head and left.

I took the package back inside. Based on its size and weight ... No doubt about it. It had to be the topaz. *Great! That's one thing down.*

Feeling re-energized, I almost skipped back into the living room. I put it down and grinned at Ronan, who was waiting in the doorway. "Ready for another round?"

By the time I needed to head home, Tara and Phillip hadn't returned yet.

Since there wasn't much else to do, I'd be going to school as normal over the coming days. The less I gave Mom cause to worry, the better. Besides, I had another appointment with Dr. Steinberg tomorrow. Based on how our last session had gone, she'd undoubtedly have more questions.

I spent the evening researching for spas that were a decent drive away but still worth going, consulting with Jack via text. Before long, we found the perfect place, offering an all-inclusive spa experience with lots of extra stuff with words I didn't know the meaning of, and was pretty sure I didn't *want* to know. It was only a three-hour drive away with a direct bus that came through town only a few times a week. It was perfect.

We bought the spots for our moms, and I printed off the ticket for mine before dinner. I knew she had nothing planned for the weekend, so she'd have no excuse to decline the invitation. Much less since I had already paid for it … possibly breaking my bank account in the process, but it was all worth it if it meant that I didn't put her into a position of suffering again.

"Hey, honey." Mom smiled at me as I crawled down the stairs, my muscles still aching from the day's training.

I'd taken care to cover up any bruises or scratches. Tara could heal them tomorrow. No need to worry Mom.

"Hey," I said, taking in a big whiff of the delicious scents wafting through the house. "What's for dinner?"

"Lasagna. You've seemed so tense again lately." She shrugged. "I figured it might cheer you up."

I smiled at her warmly. I had the most

wonderful mother in the world. In the past, before Halastaesia, I'd never been able to appreciate everything she'd done for me, but now ... Now it was all crystal clear. I couldn't ask for anyone better.

"Thanks!"

We sat down together. She'd even set the table already. Normally I'd try to help out with this part, but I'd missed that window today.

"How was school?" she asked after the first bite of that savory mixture of cheese and tomato.

"Normal, I think."

I had no reason to think otherwise, after all. I certainly didn't think Corrupted Ones had appeared there in my absence.

"Well that's good. And things are going well?"

I nodded.

Our plan was progressing nicely at least. Having the Halastaesians here was making things go a lot more smoothly. I didn't know what I'd do without them in this situation. I'd be a sitting duck, just waiting for my past to catch up with me, ignorant of how to prepare for it.

We kept the mundane small talk going while we finished our meal. Then, before she could make a move, I jumped up to clear the table.

"Would you like a coffee?" I asked as I took away her plate.

"Oh, honey, no. I couldn't sleep if I had coffee now."

"A cup of tea, then?" I ventured.

She cupped my cheek with a hand. "Peppermint would be lovely. Thank you."

Moments later, I arrived back in with two steaming cups of peppermint tea. Mom was still sitting in the same spot, though she was checking emails on her phone. After placing the tea on the table in front of her, I wrapped my arms around her from behind, resting my chin on the top of her head in a childish gesture of affection.

She laughed. "What are you doing?"

"It's comfy," I growled, smirking though she couldn't see it. "And I want to give you something. But you can't look at me."

"Aww, don't be embarrassed. You used to give me things all the time."

"Yeah, when I was five. I'm sixteen now."

She tilted her head back to look at me, forcing me to lift my chin.

"And already growing up into a fine young man."

I grimaced. "Mom!"

That only elicited a laugh from her. It was nice to see her like this. Happy, without fear or pain, even if it was only for a short while. More than ever, I felt assured in my decision to give her this vacation to keep her from ever knowing about my leaving for a short while again. I wanted to protect that smile. The same way I knew she wanted to protect me. And so I had to keep the mages and Corrupted Ones from ever crossing over again, and keep her from finding out in the first place.

"I said no looking at me!"

Obediently, she lowered her head again. I slipped the printout for the info sheet and reservation for the spa from my pocket and slid it onto the table in front of her.

She studied it for a moment, and I could feel the confusion emanating for her.

"I wanted to give you something nice," I said quietly. "Because you've been looking out for me this whole time. And because I didn't want you to have to be on your own, Jack's mom is going with you. I'd have gone myself, but you know I wouldn't do well in a place like that."

I grimaced at the thought.

Mom lifted a hand and touched the reservation.

"Ben ..." Her voice trailed off. "Honey, I don't ... I—"

"You have to go," I insisted. "You've done so much for me. Let me do this for you."

She turned her head, indecision still playing in her eyes as she looked at me, but, noticing my determination, she relented and smiled.

"You're too sweet." She sighed. "Thank you, dear. It's so kind of you to think of me like this. But..."

She glanced back at the paper. "I can't leave you all alone here."

"But, Mom!" I protested. "You've gotta go.

You need a break, and you certainly deserve one. I'll be fine, I promise."

I squeezed her hand. "And besides, it's already paid for. It'll be fine."

She hesitated, but shook her head regardless.

"I'll reimburse you the money, honey. But I can't leave you all alone. If your dad could come home this weekend, it would be a different story, but …"

Okay, I saw her qualms. Time to squash them.

I took a seat next to her, never letting go of her hand.

"Mom, you've been through enough. Please, let me do this for you. If you're still worried for me, how about we see if Dr. Steinberg would agree to check up on me? As my psychologist, she knows everything that's been going on with me, and she'll have the best handle on what to do if anything happens. And I promise to check in with you on a regular basis." By using timed messages that would just send for whenever I scheduled them.

She bit her lip. She wanted to say yes. She wanted to accept my gift. I could see it. But her concern for me was still stronger.

Still, I kept a hold of both her gaze and her hand, and after a long moment, she finally relented.

"I'll speak with Dr. Steinberg. If she agrees to it, I'll go. But only if I get an hourly check-in from you, alright?"

I squinted my eyes at her. "Every five hours."
"Three."
"Deal."
Thank god for online scheduling.

CHAPTER 19

School was … odd. I'd decided to go, if only because there was nothing for me to do at Jack's place except get beat up by Ronan. While I could use the training, I couldn't miss too many days of school. Even if the teachers didn't think it was fishy, someone else might. Someone like Harvey, who wasn't exactly my biggest fan right now. When he was mad, he could be unpredictable.

We ran into each other on the way to class, but he turned his head away abruptly, like a thirteen-year-old girl fighting with her best friend. I didn't bother commenting. He'd made his position clear: he wouldn't so much as listen to my explanations. I sort of understood where he was coming from, but he should know me better than that.

Nevertheless, I took my seat next to him in chemistry. We were lab partners and today was experiment time.

Harvey did an excellent job ignoring me while we listened to the teacher's run through, though I didn't exactly try very hard to make myself be noticed.

Soon enough, the handouts were distributed, and Harvey and I were forced to interact.

"I'll get the chemicals, so you set up the burner," Harvey decided briskly. He wasn't even looking me in the eye.

I wordlessly complied.

Truthfully, I had never expected him to be this mad at me. I wondered how I would feel if the roles were reversed—if I'd seen him with a different girl than Cindy. I'd have given him a talking to, sure. Heck, if Vivienne had felt strongly about it, it might have even made me mad enough to punch him. But the way he was behaving now wasn't like him. Like us.

We started the experiment, only speaking the bare minimum to coordinate our actions and discuss the reactions we saw. Okay, so maybe he needed me to take the first step. Maybe he was just finding it difficult to bridge the gap.

"Hey, Harvey," I said, as I poured nitric acid into the beaker, "are you going to the rally tomorrow?"

Vivienne had warned us yesterday that she needed to attend it after school and would be missing out on training as a result. Since Cindy was on the cheer squad as well, I figured it was reasonable to assume that Harvey would be going. Which might just give me the perfect chance to patch things up with him. It felt wrong leaving to go to Halastaesia without having made things right with him. After all, there was still a possibility that we would fail. That *I* would fail. And I had a strong feeling that failure, in this case, was synonymous with death.

Harvey shrugged, not taking his eyes off the beaker.

I stopped pouring—the color of the tincture looked like it matched the diagram on our sheet.

"How are things going with Cindy, anyway?" I continued my quest.

He sneered at me, meeting my gaze for just a split second to show me pure disdain.

"What do *you* care?" he asked.

Oof. This was going to be way harder than I'd anticipated.

"Well, last time I checked you were my friend, and I tend to care about how things are going for them, you know."

He only scoffed and turned back to the handout, reaching for the next chemical to be added to the mix. I shook my head in exasperation. Why was he being so stubborn?

We continued with the experiment in silence, not meeting each other's eyes. I was annoyed at him for being difficult, and he was annoyed at me about Tara, I assumed. Had high school always been this full of drama? I certainly didn't remember it being like this before Halastaesia.

Everything had been so much easier back then. So much more boring. I almost wished it could go back to that time, if only because it had been simpler.

After a long time of silence, while he was stirring the beaker with a slim glass rod, he finally spoke up again.

"You know, you changed."

I glanced up from the swirling, colored fluid to look at him, but my eye was drawn to something just behind him, something that didn't quite want to come into focus.

"You used to be different, somehow. I mean, before. And I get it. Something pretty terrible happened to you."

The hairs on my arms and neck were rising up, standing, electrified with the charge that was emanating from behind Harvey. It was no more than a glimmer in the air, but I saw it. I felt it.

"But it's like I don't even know you anymore. You used to tell me stuff. We used to be buddies."

I squinted, trying to bring the vague shape into focus.

"I used to know what's going on in your head. We were on the same page about things."

My fists were clenched, and even though I felt freezing cold, I could feel sweat drench my shirt and hair.

"But now, I don't know. It's like my buddy's on holiday or something, and someone else has taken his place. Someone who ..."

The shape was moving closer. I recognized it. Even though I couldn't see it clearly, there was no doubt in my mind about what I was facing. And it was here, in my classroom.

"Sorry for saying this, but someone who can be a bit cuckoo at times."

A Corrupted One.

It was approaching slowly. But how? The mages couldn't possibly have worked fast enough to break through again, could they?

"Maybe I'm just not cut out for this, maybe I'm in the wrong here, I don't know."

Then again, this Corrupted One clearly wasn't all here yet. It was like a phantom, a ghost. Affecting anything physically right now was probably out of the question for it, but nevertheless, every fiber of my body was tense as I watched its every movement.

"But I really don't think I can be your friend anymore, Ben."

It saw me. It knew I was here. But like me, it was biding its time. I shuffled closer, but without ever getting close enough to touch. This had to stop. Now.

"Ben, are you listening to me? Ben?"

"Leave!" I shouted at the Corrupted One. "And tell your masters … I. Will. Shut. Them. Down!"

As I jumped from my seat to deliver the threat, I swept the beaker off the table and it shattered on the floor into a thousand pieces. My attention was diverted from the Corrupted One as droplets of splash back hit the bare skin around my ankles.

They burned. I'd felt worse agony before, but the realization of what I'd just done still hit me like a trainwreck.

The next few moments passed by like a blur—the teacher came running over, wiping off acidic droplets on my skin and clothes, while one of my female classmates raced to get a first aid kit.

Still in shock, I looked for the Corrupted One, but it was gone. Instead, my gaze met Harvey's, and everything he had said finally registered with me.

I'd just sealed the end of our friendship.

Somehow, I managed to convince the medics who came rushing to the school to check my acid burns to not call my mom, though I had no idea how I succeeded. By any rights, the school, at the very least, had the obligation to inform her of what had happened. But they didn't.

And so, after spending the rest of the school day in the doctor's office with medics treating my burns, I was finally allowed to leave.

My injuries weren't severe. There were some circular holes in my skin where the flesh was exposed, but my teacher had reacted quickly enough that the acid hadn't had the time to eat its way too deeply. I was used to handling pain far worse than this. Halastaesia had toughened me up quite a bit.

So I left my bike at school and took the bus to go see Dr. Steinberg.

Being early, I uneasily settled down in the waiting room. My eyes kept flitting to the door and the windows, despite knowing that mundane entryways held no meaning for other-dimensional beings crossing the borders of existence. I would have preferred to go straight back to Jack's place and talk to Tara, Ronan, and Phillip, but I needed to make sure Dr. Steinberg was on board with this weekend. And if she was, I needed to make sure that she wouldn't call my mother straight away if I disappeared for a few days.

This was something I needed to take care of, Corrupted Ones appearing again or not. It was for my mom's sake.

Still, I pulled out my phone and texted Jack.

Corrupted Ones are already starting to appear again.

He'd tell the others. Based on how long it took between the shadows materializing the first time, and fully transitioning, we should have several weeks before the mages were ready again, but I had the odd feeling that they'd be faster this time around, if only because this time they knew exactly how to do it, having accomplished it once before. But how much did that affect the timeline? Might they start breaking through again tomorrow, or only a few days from now? How much time did the mages really need?

A shadow moved past the milky glass door, and after a moment, Dr. Steinberg's secretary peeked in. "She's ready for you now."

I made my way to Dr. Steinberg's office. She was sitting in her usual chair, her back straight, her expression composed. There were no signs of the nervousness she'd portrayed the last time I'd been to see her.

"Hello, Ben." She smiled at me.

"Hi."

I took my seat.

"Your mother called to tell me about your present. I agreed to check in on you while she's away. But I hope you realize that this isn't a service I would normally provide."

She raised an eyebrow at me.

"You think I'm at risk," I acknowledged. Judging by the way she was holding herself, she must have worked through the anxiety from last time. She must have rationalized away what she'd seen. Which meant that as far as we were concerned, she thought that the alleged gasses had regressed any progress I had made.

"It doesn't matter what I think," she said, smiling slightly. "What matters is what *you* think. And you were the one who suggested that I look after you, according to your mother."

I nodded, my mind racing. With her no longer

believing that the Corrupted Ones were real, how could I convince her not to call for my mother if I disappeared?

"Why is that?" She tilted her head to one side, observing me.

Her expression gave away nothing of what she was thinking. How bad did she think my state really was?

"I figured that if something happened again, you would know best how to deal with it. You know my history, and what's going on in my head. If I stayed with a friend, they or their parents might be overwhelmed or panic if something happened."

"What do you think might happen?"

I hesitated, and the memory of chemistry class this morning flashed through my mind. I moved my legs to hide as much of them from Dr. Steinberg's sight as possible, the bandages in particular.

"Nothing," I said, just a little too quickly.

Her eyes moved down to my ankles, and just for a moment, they narrowed.

"Benjamin," she said gently yet firmly, blinking back up at me, "what happened?"

Crap. I'd given myself away by trying to hide it.

Well, no point in keeping it secret now. She could easily find out by calling the school. Or the hospital.

I grimaced. "I had a little accident in chemistry

class and splashed some acid on myself."

She crossed her legs. "Why don't you tell me about it in a little more detail?"

And so I told her. Well ... mostly. I told her about Harvey and our conversation, but I left out the Corrupted One. Instead, I made it seem like I had just reacted to what Harvey had said.

"And how do you feel about that?" she asked, her head tilting to one side compassionately. "Your friend telling you these things?"

I shrugged. Truthfully, it sucked big time, but I had bigger problems right now.

"I mean, there's nothing I can do, is there? He thinks I've changed. And I agree. I *have* changed. I think I've become a better version of myself. But he would rather I revert to how I used to be. To how I was before my accident. So what can I do? I won't pretend that I'm someone I'm not."

"You're defensive," Dr. Steinberg said.

"No, I'm not."

"Then you're angry."

I frowned. "Angry? Why would I be angry?"

Dr. Steinberg didn't respond. Instead, she looked down at her notes, studying them for a moment.

"Why did you knock over the acid?"

My frown deepened. "It was an accident."

Her gaze shot up to meet mine, and it was intense, almost akin to a glare. "You reacted very strongly to Harvey saying that he was no longer interested in continuing your friendship. You jumped up, shouted, and knocked over a beaker. And yet, now you claim not to be angry."

Okay. Time to come up with a reasonable explanation. I couldn't very well tell her now that all her examples of my anger stemmed from my reaction to a Corrupted One.

I cast down my eyes.

"It was an accident," I growled. "But I guess I am a little angry."

"Why?"

"Because it's so easy for him to just throw me aside. To just decide that after everything I've been through, I'm not fun enough anymore to hang out with. About his snap judgements without letting me explain myself. For being a bad friend since the moment I woke up from my coma."

The moment I started talking, more and more examples came to mind. More and more reasons why I had every right to be angry at Harvey. His dismissal of my time in Halastaesia, his dismissal of what happened at the carnival. His dismissal of my anxiety, my paranoia—even though it had proven to be right—his lack of interest in what I had to say.

I *was* angry. I hadn't noticed before, because I'd been busy thinking of how to save two worlds, but everything he'd done and hadn't done … it piled up and created a mountain of resentment. Resentment I had denied up to this point.

After I let it all out, I breathed deeply. It felt

like talking about it had actually made my chest a little lighter.

"How do you feel now?"

"Better," I admitted. "I didn't realize how much this was weighing on me."

"Then I'd like to talk to you about guilt now."

"Guilt?" I blinked at her, bewildered. "What guilt?"

"The feeling of guilt is something that will often make us act irrationally, or react more extreme than we normally would, and in this session, I've seen two separate sources of guilt in you."

"You have?" I squinted, trying to think of what she could possibly be referring to.

"You can't see them?" she returned the question, peering at me.

I was at a loss for words.

After a moment of silence, Dr. Steinberg shifted in her seat.

"You gave your mother a very luxurious, expensive gift. Why?"

So she doesn't notice when I'm gone. So she won't worry again. So she won't have to experience the same sense of loss as she did before.

But I didn't say any of that.

"She's been so great and went through so much because of me. I wanted to thank her. To do something nice for her."

"Is that something you would have thought of doing before your accident?"

I shook my head. "Probably not."

"Why not? What's different?"

Now it clicked. I realized what Dr. Steinberg was referring to, and she wasn't wrong. I had been acting much kinder toward my mom. I'd tried to make sure to be a good son, to spare her any more pain. To show her how much I loved and appreciated her in a way that would have never occurred to me way back when.

"Guilt," I admitted, smiling crookedly. "She suffered a lot because of me, and I see it every time she worries about me. The fear comes back. It still haunts her. She's terrified that something like that might happen again. And I feel guilty about it. It's my fault that she has panic attacks sometimes. It kinda looks like some sort of PTSD, to be honest. And I just … I wish I could turn back time and make sure she never has to feel that pain. I want to go back to past her and just tell her that everything's gonna be okay. But I can't. So I want to make sure that the present her knows it, instead."

Dr. Steinberg nodded almost imperceptibly, satisfied, and jotted down a few things. "And why do you feel guilt toward Harvey?"

"Harvey?" My head shot up. "What makes you think I feel guilty about him?"

Dr. Steinberg awarded me the tiniest smile. "You just told me all the things that made you angry about his behavior, yet until this morning, you never made any attempt to show that anger.

Or to confront him about it. Why do you think that is?"

I chuckled. "You think it's because I feel guilty?"

She didn't say anything.

"Look, he's been an ass, but he used to be an ass before, too. What's different is that I've changed. I can hardly blame him for not having had a life-altering accident like I did, can I?"

"In what way do you feel like your accident has changed you from who you were before … in particular, in relation to your friendship?"

I took a moment to think about her question.

My hands closed around the edge of my leather seat, feeling the soft, warm, skin-like fabric. What was it with offices and leather chairs anyway? Were they so common because they looked classy, or was there another reason?

My gaze traveled slowly around the room as though I hoped to find the answer to her question among the various seemingly random objects around the room. I'd always thought that for a psychologist's office, it was a remarkably comfortable place. Before I'd come, I'd always expected to find a very cold, clinical place. But instead, I saw a bowl with stress balls, a framed, child's drawing of a smiling sunflower, a lava lamp that seemed to always be on when I came, and a number of books—some with serious titles clearly relating to the study of the mind, others more like self-help books. My gaze rested on the lava lamp, watching the bubbles move up and down, squishing past one another whenever they crossed paths, before being assimilated in one of the two pools of colored chemicals.

Harvey.

Did I feel guilty? But about what? Sure, Dr. Steinberg had taken her assumption from my story where I'd changed some important key aspects, but her words didn't feel all wrong. It was like they'd awoken something in me.

She was right.

No matter how often Harvey hadn't been there for me lately, I'd never held it against him. Instead, I'd just accepted it. Why? I wouldn't have before. Heck, before I might have been the one ending our friendship after being disregarded so many times.

He'd been a bad friend for a long time now. But somehow ... I'd felt like *I'd* been the bad friend.

"He was there that day," I eventually said, quietly. "The day of my accident. He saw it happen."

Dr. Steinberg didn't interrupt me, not even when I paused to find the right words.

"I can't imagine how horrible that must've been. I could imagine that it might have given him some kind of trauma. I'm sure it would've happened to me, if our roles had been reversed." I chuckled, sadly. "Mom told me that he was there at the hospital a lot while I was gone. He came by every other day. But then, when I woke up, I was a different person to the one he'd lost. I experienced so many things in Halastaesia. I grew as a person. By a lot. I mean, I had to.

"I do think I changed for the better. I'm more conscious of the people around me than I was before. I see the value of the things and people in my life now. But that turned me into someone else. And all the while he stayed the same. How can I blame him for that? But it's kind of like ... I took something away from him by changing. I took away the person who was his best friend and substituted him with myself. Like my mom, he went through a lot. And all he wanted was his friend back, but instead, he got ... me."

PART IV

CHAPTER 20

I left Dr. Steinberg's office feeling very somber, before getting on the bus home. On the way, I only looked out the window, watching the world pass by in a blur. Dr. Steinberg had been very happy with the progress we'd made. I, on the other hand, didn't know how I felt about it.

The guilt I felt for Mom was more tangible, more understandable. But I hadn't realized that the same had been true for Harvey. Now that I did, I wasn't sure what to do about it. He'd essentially told me to get lost, and I was sure my episode this morning did little to change that. What was the point in forcing a friendship if we weren't on the same page anymore? We'd become two different people, and he'd probably done the best thing for him by severing our ties. Who was I to question that and force myself back onto him? If we could truly be friends again, it would happen. We were still lab partners. Still classmates. There'd be a lot of time to mend our broken relationship once I'd beaten the mages.

I'd taken the bus to Jack's house, figuring that my text message from earlier probably required some explanation. Mom wouldn't be home for another few hours anyway, so she wouldn't worry—provided the school had kept their word and not called her. One glance at my phone showed no news from her, but instead twelve new messages from Jack and Vivienne.

Even before I rang the doorbell, I could hear grunts of fighting from inside. But it was the sounds of sparring, not the noises of a real fight.

Phillip opened the door, looking remarkably bored.

"You're late," he grumbled.

"And I need to head off now," Vivienne said, pushing past him. Her blonde hair was tied into a neat bun and not a single strand was out of place. Still, her cheeks showed the healthy flush of a girl who'd just done some physical exercise. She was already wearing her cheerleader's uniform, a gym bag strapped on her arm.

She put a hand around the back of my neck and gave me a quick peck on the lips before pushing out.

"I'll call you later, okay?" She smiled, squeezing my hand.

"Sure. Have fun at training!"

The door fell into lock behind her, and I followed Phillip out into the back where Jack and Ronan were sparring, Tara watching with keen interest. As soon as I stepped out, they all paused and diverted their attention to me.

Tara jumped up and immediately stepped toward me. "You saw one?"

"This morning, in chemistry class. It wasn't fully there, not even half, but I saw it. And sensed it. And," I added, with a sigh, "I might have caused a mild commotion because of it. Kinda lost my cool."

Tara frowned at me, her hazel eyes full of concern. Then, her frown deepened as she studied me.

"You're injured," she recognized. "You're in pain."

Leave it to a healer flower fae to read the things I tried to hide in my aura.

"Where?"

I knew that look in her eyes. It was the kind that didn't accept any excuse, retort, or needless acts of heroism.

Defeated, I sat down on one of the garden chairs and pulled up my pant legs to reveal the bandages. In an instant, Tara had dropped to her knees beside me and unraveled them.

Even the tiniest movement of the fabric against the burned places stung, but I managed to keep my wincing to a minimum. Jack fared a little worse. He visibly flinched when Tara exposed my wounds.

Ronan whistled through his teeth.

"That looks nasty," he commented flippantly.

"How'd you manage that?"

"Chemistry," I sighed. "I splashed some acid on myself when the Corrupted One showed up. It's just lucky I didn't accidentally hurt anyone else."

Tara was already running her hands up and down my calves, and I could feel the familiar, soothing energy of her healing power seeping into my skin, repairing the damage. It prickled, and hurt a little, but much less than the actual injury did. After a few moments, my legs were as good as new.

"Status report?" I asked, glancing at Jack when Tara was done.

He shrugged. "Bowl's not done yet. Tara's been getting the rest of the ritual set up though."

I gnawed on the inside of my cheek. "So the bowl's the last piece ... Alright, well, I guess there's not much else we can do for the moment."

I sighed and took his hand to help me to my feet.

"I'd better head home. My mom should get back soon."

"Wait." Tara stepped in my way. "The Corrupted One, how much had it manifested?"

"Not very. It was different from before though. It saw me. It moved toward me. But it was barely present on this plane of existence. It's kind of like ... opposite to how it was before, you know? Last time it looked like their bodies were getting here first, and then their minds followed. But now … Its mind was here. The body wasn't."

She nodded, seriously, taking in everything I said. Then she stepped out of my way.

"Be careful," she said, and I left.

"Hey, Mom, I'm home," I called into the door when I got back.

"I'm here, honey," she said, her voice heavy with sadness and suppressed hope.

I wasn't sure why I knew this, but I did. It sounded far too familiar. It evoked the urge to run to her side and hold her tight, to stop her from crying.

I closed the door and rushed inside to find her.

She must've found out about the accident at school and thrown herself into a worrying fit. But if that was the case, why wasn't she already at the door, throwing herself at me? And why hadn't my phone blown up with messages and calls from her?

Not only that, I couldn't figure out where she was. She'd sounded so close, but as I covered the entire ground floor of the house, I couldn't find her anywhere.

"Mom?" I called out.

No response.

"Where are you?"

She didn't reply. Equal parts confused and worried, I ran up to the second floor, but she was nowhere to be found there either. It was only then that I remembered that the front door had been locked. She wouldn't have locked it if she'd been inside. *Which could only mean that I must have imagined hearing her.*

Or, as the thought rushing after the first one suggested, *someone mimicked her.* Making me believe that I was hearing her.

I stopped running around and calmed my breathing, while slowly looking around myself. So far, I couldn't make out any traces of someone or something else being here, but that didn't mean a thing. The mages could do a lot of things; they might have learned a few new tricks since my time in Halastaesia.

As I was listening to the world around me, focusing in on every tick of the clock, on every groan from the stretching of the wood, on every clicking in the radiators, my arms covered in goosebumps as my hairs stood up, the quiet sound of a key in the front door reached my senses. I moved to the landing, dropping into a fight ready stance before my mind had even caught up.

The door swung open to reveal … Mom. Mom carrying several shopping bags. Once my first bout of surprise passed, I lunged forward to take some of the bags off of her.

"Oh! Hi, Ben! I didn't think you'd be home yet."

"Hey, Mom. Yeah, I thought I should catch up on some homework. Got a test next week."

I really must have imagined it then, hearing her when I came in.

"Look at you, being all studious! Just wait 'til your dad hears this."

I grimaced.

"You don't have to tell him every time I study a little, you know," I grumbled, but she only chuckled to herself.

"Alright then, off you go." She shooed me out of the kitchen like a gosling. "Go study. I'll call you when dinner is ready."

I rolled my eyes at her, but obediently went up the stairs to my room. Seeing as it was my cover story, and I really didn't have anything better to do, I decided to actually do some studying. It sure wouldn't do me any harm.

Pulling out my physics book, I focused on reading the chapter, doing my best to draw connections between what I read to what I knew and could observe. I was actually pulled into the material quite a bit, but before long, I snapped back to reality suddenly.

The hairs all along my body stood on end, and shivers ran up and down my spine as my skin crawled. All of my senses were heightened in an instant, and my heart was beating fast, making every sound thrice as loud, and every moment jump into my vision like a light in the darkness.

I wasn't alone anymore. Slowly looking around my room, I pushed my chair back. Where were they? This wasn't Tara. No. This energy was something much more sinister. Another Corrupted One. And the fact that I could feel its presence like this did not bode well for us.

I grabbed an old baseball club from junior high, tensing my muscles, preparing myself for whatever might be to come.

"Come on out," I growled into the quiet room.

Only the ticking of the clock, irritatingly loud and annoying, disrupted the otherwise absolute silence.

"Where are you?"

My gaze glided across every wall and surface in the room, but I didn't see so much as a glimmer in the air. And yet, I knew it had to be here somewhere. I stared into the shadows until my eyes were burning, but nothing.

"Show yourself!"

I took a single step forward, and by chance, glanced down at the floor.

There it was, only its face peeking out through the floor, grinning up at me with its terrible, finger-long, triangular teeth. And then, as if it had only been waiting for me to notice it, the Corrupted One in the floor closed its jaws around my ankle, sinking its razor-sharp fangs into my flesh.

I yelped out in pain, while doing my best to blindly beat at its head, and eyes in particular, with my bat. The moment its jaws released my leg, I dropped forward, onto the floor. My leg wouldn't sustain my weight anymore. I hurled myself around, poising the bat, lest the Corrupted One should take my moment of weakness and use the opening to attack, but it was gone. Seconds later, however, the door to my room burst open and Mom rushed in, frying pan still in hand. She dropped it to the floor in a loud bang when she saw me sprawled across the floor. Her eyes flitted to my ankles, and she grew pale. I hadn't checked my wound yet myself, but it had to be nasty.

Dropping to the floor next to me, she pulled up the rest of my trouser leg, leading my own gaze down to my ankle. The horrifying gory look I'd expected wasn't what I found, though. It still looked nasty, of course, really terrible, but not from having had a monster's teeth yank out half of it. No.

What I saw was a leg that had been splashed by acid.

I stared at it, confused. Tara had healed this only an hour ago. I'd watched her do it. So how had the Corrupted One undone it? Could they rewind time on a person's body? Was this another trick of the mages? Another way to fight me?

Mom's hands flew to cover her mouth as she

gazed at all the damage to my leg. Truthfully, it hadn't seemed this bad in school. It certainly hadn't hurt as much as this, though once the shock wore off, it once more turned into a painful throb rather than a sharp ache.

"Ben," she said, her voice quiet as a mouse and shaky like a badly constructed church spire. "What the hell happened?"

Her eyes flitted to mine, fear and suppressed anger mixed with helplessness domineering her gaze.

"I …" I tried to find an explanation. For myself, not for her. How had the mages managed to undo Tara's healing spell? If they could do that, what else were they capable of? They shouldn't have been able to do this. "I had an accident at school."

I avoided her gaze, and my eyes fell on my bag which had been toppled over, contents spilling out across the floor. There was a small box and a folded piece of paper I didn't remember putting in there.

"What kind of accident?" Her voice was shaking.

I took her hand, to reassure her, but not only was it trembling, it was also ice cold. After a second, she pulled it from my grasp.

"What kind of accident?" she repeated.

My eyes kept being drawn to the little purple plastic box. I needed to know what that was. It felt important. Very important.

"I had a fight with Harvey," I mumbled, reaching for it. "And some chemicals got knocked over."

"He attacked you with chemicals?" She was almost screeching.

I shook my head, just as my hands closed around the box.

"I accidentally knocked it over. The vial dropped to the floor, and I was hit by the splash."

It was a pill box. A small pill box with twenty-eight compartments in four rows. Two rows had long, white and red pills in them. The others small, flat, round ones. One of each were empty already.

What the …

Mom took a deep breath. "Why wasn't I called? And why didn't you say anything? You should be in the hospital for god's sake!"

While her worry wasn't gone completely, it was turning to anger now, and rightfully so. I glanced at the unfamiliar folded sheet of paper, and started to reach for it as I responded.

"I didn't want to worry you, so I asked them not to say anything. The medics came and they treated me, I should be fine. I don't know why the pain just started again. It hasn't been hurting at all since I left school."

Mom snatched the piece of paper before I could get to it. Glaring at me, she opened it and read. Then she gave it back to me.

"Looks like you haven't taken your second dose of painkillers and antibiotics yet."

I looked at her, then glanced at the paper. This wasn't mine. I'd never seen it or the pillbox before in my life. And yet, the handwriting describing how and when I should take the pills in the box was unmistakably mine. But … how?

Without another word, Mom got to her feet and left. I used the respite I was given to haul myself onto my bed, trying to rely as little as possible on my legs, and making sure not to brush my ankles against anything. They hurt enough even without added irritation.

A moment later, Mom reentered my room, only to place a glass of water on my nightstand.

"Take your pills," she growled. "And after, we are going to have a talk."

She left again, but I could feel her anger lingering, even after she slammed the door and trampled down the stairs. I'd be scared of what awaited me in that conversation if I wasn't so confused by what had actually happened.

Those pills weren't mine. Neither was that note, and yet, I must have written it. Tara had healed my wounds, and yet, here they were, looking the exact same as they had this morning when I'd received them. And there had been another Corrupted One. The second one today. And whatever it had done to me, it had brought my wounds and all the pain back to me.

None of it made any sense.

More than anything else, it meant I was no longer safe in my own home. The mages had sent it. They knew where I lived. They knew where I spent my days. They had figured out a way to attack me.

And if they could attack me, then Mom was in harm's way, too. If they were as smart as they thought themselves, they knew she was my weak spot. After all, she didn't believe Halastaesia was real. And she wasn't like Vivienne either, able to defend herself from something coming at her.

I straightened my jaw, pills in hand, looking at them. They looked legitimate enough. I doubted the mages knew enough of my world to mimic our medicine so convincingly. Which meant that they'd probably done something to my memories instead. Which, admittedly, wasn't a comforting thought. What else had they altered?

Making up my mind, I gulped down the pills with some water.

This needed to end soon.

This weekend. In three days, the real fight could begin. But first, I needed to do all I could to reassure Mom and soothe her righteous anger.

I took one last careful look around my room, before I left to slink down the stairs and meet Mom in the dining room.

CHAPTER 21

I felt like a guilty party entering court with Mom's grave looks following me as I took my seat across from her at the table. Her expression didn't twitch—it was a mask of perfect, grave indifference. Her hands were folded on the table in front of her, no tremble in sight. Truthfully, it felt like I hadn't seen her this composed since before my accident.

Silence spread out between us, only disturbed by the ticking of the clock on the wall and the soft clicking of the heating kicking in.

"You're grounded," she eventually said, very matter of fact. "And that should give us ample time for communication."

I didn't mind being grounded. At least not after this weekend. I didn't respond.

"That being said, you'd better start talking now, mister. I want to know *exactly* what happened this morning. And then I want you to explain to me why you kept it from me."

I didn't bother with hesitation. Her anger was justified. As my mother, she should have been the first person to find out about this. This was a calm, brooding anger, the one that was most dangerous. The one that was cold and calculating. The kind that could cause real trouble and wasn't so easily appeased. A kiss and a hug wouldn't do the trick.

Dropping my gaze to the table, and marveling at its patterns of darker lines on the bright wood, I shared the same mostly true story with Mom that I'd shared with Dr. Steinberg. Consistency was best. Less likely to cause a trip-up.

While I told my story, my mom's jaw hardened as she clenched her teeth. Her fingers and knuckles grew whiter with every spoken word as well.

Then, when I finished, she let out a long breath. "Alright. And why did you try to keep it secret?"

I was the one fumbling with my hands now.

Because you would have thought I was crazy if I told you the truth.

No, not just that.

Because I didn't want you to worry. Not again. Not anymore.

I directed my gaze up at the ceiling, hoping to find the words there. A script of some sort, spelled out from my own well-hidden teleprompter so I could seem certain of my words and just get them out.

"I was talking to Dr. Steinberg about that, actually," I eventually said.

I received a sharp intake of breath in return.

"Dr. Steinberg knew?"

I nodded, and looked up at Mom. She'd grown

pale. And her brows were furrowed in both disbelief and anger. Her shoulders were beginning to tremble, too.

"Patient confidentiality," I reminded her. "She's not allowed to tell you anything if I don't want you to know."

Her shoulders relaxed the smallest amount.

"Right. Well?"

Yep, should have seen that coming.

"We were talking a lot about guilt." I bit my lip. Did I really want to lay that out there? She was my mom. What if telling her about my feeling guilty would make her feel guilty as well? That would just create a never-ending cycle of guilt and not really help anything, or anyone.

The flicker of understanding in my mom's eyes convinced me though. I needed to just tell her.

"I've caused you a lot of pain over the past year," I muttered. "I figured it was time to stop. And this," I gestured at my leg, "didn't seem like a big enough deal to bother you with. It was treated, and it's going to get better in no time, so …"

Mom reached across the table to place her hand on mine. I lifted up my gaze to meet hers. The anger was gone, replaced by her usual gentle demeanor.

"Ben."

Just my name. And yet, it was laden with meaning, conveying all she was feeling, complicated though it was.

"I'm your mother. You're *meant* to bother me with this stuff. I'm *meant* to worry about you. That's not something you need to feel guilty about."

I nodded, and a little hardness reentered her gaze.

"But you're still grounded for not telling me."

That was only fair.

"You'll still go on the trip, though, right?" I gave her my most pleading look. "Please, I don't want you to miss out on it because of me."

She hesitated, clearly having planned on skipping it, like I'd expected. I pulled my hand from her grasp and put it on top of hers instead, squeezing gently.

"Mom, please. Let me do this for you. Dr. Steinberg did agree to take responsibility. And she won't be under oath or anything during that time, so she'll let you know the second anything happens. Please?"

We had a staring contest then, neither of us willing to back down. But eventually, she cast her eyes down and sighed.

"Fine. But you're grounded over the weekend as well, don't forget that. You're only allowed to leave the house if it's literally on fire."

I smirked, as did she.

"And don't you dare burn it down intentionally," she added with a raised eyebrow.

Mom made me stay home from school the next day. She said she didn't want me to risk my wounds getting dirty or abraded by my jeans, so she took me to my GP instead, making him redress the burns. After a brief inspection, he also recommended I take it easy for a few days. I accepted everything he and Mom said with nods. I'd take it easy alright. At least until Friday. And then I wouldn't have that luxury anymore.

After getting me home from the doctor's and taking my dosage of pills for the morning, Mom headed out to go to work, leaving me lounging on the couch zapping through TV channels.

There was nothing I could do. Nothing to make the weekend come faster, and nothing to prepare myself for returning to Halastaesia. I couldn't even try to research what it was the mages wanted "back" from me, whatever it was I'd "taken". What a joke that was in the first place, considering they'd been the ones who sent me back. Against my will, I might add.

Though knowing about how my absence had affected my loved ones here, I almost wish they'd sent me back sooner. I couldn't bring myself to wish they'd never summoned me in the first place, because I had lived there for a whole year. I'd made friends, found love, found meaning and pride in myself, while learning so much about people and myself. Those weren't experiences I wanted to lose, or wish I'd never had.

So instead, I flipped from one TV station to the next, not really getting into anything. My mind was still on edge, constantly half-expecting a Corrupted One to appear again. How long would it take for one of the mages to break through?

I landed on a TV show playing in a hospital. A doctor looked critically at the unconscious patient—a boy around my age, hooked up to a bunch of machines. Two people who were probably meant to be his parents were standing there as well, looking concerned.

"He's stable," the doctor said. "But whether he'll wake up or not is a matter of his own willpower at this point. There's nothing more I can do."

When the doorbell rang, I actually flinched. After a split second of fear washing over me, I reasoned that no monster would actually ring the doorbell if they could just materialize in my floor. So I went and opened the door instead.

Vivienne was panting, wearing her cheerleading outfit, her eyes wide and her nostrils flaring in concern. As soon as she recognized me, her eyes flitted down to my ankles, and, seeing my bandages, she burst into tears.

My arms were around her before I knew what I was doing, gently pulling her inside.

"Ben," she cried, her arms clutching at my back as she buried her face in my chest.

I softly stroked the back of her head.

"I just heard …"

"It's okay," I soothed her. "I'm okay, I promise."

"You got burned by *acid*!"

"I know. But it's really okay. I'm fine."

Her small frame trembled under my hands.

"What happened?" she eventually asked, peeking up at me with tear-smeared eyes. Well, if I couldn't be honest with her, there was no hope left.

"I saw a Corrupted One. In the classroom."

I didn't know what I'd expected, but a look of complete and utter confusion and lack of understanding wasn't it.

"One of those monsters," I reminded her. "Like at the carnival."

I supposed I couldn't blame her for not immediately making the connection. She hadn't been fighting them like I had, after all.

"Right."

Then she buried her face in my chest again. She was still trembling, but the crying had faded, at least. After a few minutes, she calmed down again.

"I should go," she said quietly to my chest. "I snuck off campus during lunch but … I need to be back for the rally."

"Of course. Good luck out there. I hope you have fun!"

She looked up at me and nodded.

Her leaving left a weird feeling in my chest. It felt like something wasn't quite right, but I couldn't put a finger on it. Something about this situation felt odd. Almost as if I was stuck in some bad TV show, being filmed or watched from the corners of my vision.

Which could only mean one thing.

The mages had their eye on me. They were observing me, somehow. I had learned to trust my instincts in Halastaesia, so I trusted them not to let me down. It made me all the more glad that Vivienne had left. I didn't want her to be in their vision alongside me. It would only put her in harm's way.

Knowing that there was nothing I could do to stop them watching, I decided to let them believe I hadn't noticed. Acting like a normal, bored teenager was the most likely story they'd believe. It was what would rouse the least suspicion.

So I returned to the TV, which was still playing, but instead of the tragic hospital drama, I found myself returning to a sports show.

Sentenced to stay home from school for the rest of the week, I felt like a sitting duck. I was a stationary target, unable to leave the house except to go to my therapy session with Dr. Steinberg, which was moved up on Thursday, to accommodate my mom's schedule. She insisted on driving me there, not wanting me to strain my leg unless I had to.

Honestly, I felt she was being overly cautious. It was just a burn and it had been treated. I was taking pills to numb the pain and antibiotics to prevent infection. As far as I was concerned, normal, cautious use should not be out of the question.

But I let her have her way, without argument. If this made her feel more at ease, so be it.

"Hello, Ben." Dr. Steinberg smiled at me. "How are you feeling?"

"I'm good," I said.

"Hello, Dr. Steinberg." My Mom stepped in. "Thank you so much for agreeing to this weekend. I know it's a far cry from anything that could be expected from you as part of your role."

"It is, but … I have taken a personal interest in Ben's situation." Dr. Steinberg hesitated for a moment, before she closed the door and gestured for Mom to take a seat beside me.

"There is actually something I wanted to discuss with you both. Keeping in mind that your answer will have absolutely no bearing on our agreement for this weekend, or further treatment of Ben's condition, with your permission, I would like to write a paper about this treatment. About Ben's situation, and, of course, with complete anonymity."

She paused for a moment, looking from Mom to me.

"This paper wouldn't really be touched by the wider public … it would merely be included in a scientific journal, read by other professionals and enthusiasts."

"Absolutely not." Mom's response had come faster than I had expected, though I wasn't surprised about her reaction.

Dr, Steinberg nodded, unfazed. "Very well."

Then she smiled at me. "So, Ben, let's pick up where we left off last time, shall we?"

I averted my gaze to look at my mom. "Mom."

She looked at me, and I raised an eyebrow.

"It wouldn't do any harm. No one would know it's me. And it's not like anyone in this town would ever read it. Dr. Steinberg's done so much for me. For us."

Okay, cards on the table—I wasn't overly thrilled to have my mental condition laid out in black and white. Then again, it wouldn't do me any harm, either. Besides, whatever Dr. Steinberg wrote, would be only her interpretation of the truth, not the actual reality, considering how much I kept from her these days. And it might advance her career. She *had* helped me quite a bit, if not exactly in the ways she might think. I felt like I owed her that much, at least. She'd been a confidante, if nothing else, over the last few months. Someone who I could talk to about Halastaesia as much as I needed and wanted. Someone who didn't tell me after every sentence that I was imagining things, someone who didn't dismiss my feelings, and thoughts on the matter, but took them into account with everything she said to me. Yes, it was just a job for her. I was just another client who paid her for doing exactly that. But that didn't change the fact that I was grateful for her having been around. Another doctor might not have acted the way she did.

"Honey," Mom drawled, "are you sure? Once it's out there, you can't take it back."

I met her gaze steadily. "It's fine."

Mom didn't respond, but the little movement in the corner of her mouth told me her answer. She was leaving it up to me.

"You can write it," I said to Dr. Steinberg. "I don't mind."

A twinkle entered her eyes as she nodded. "If, at any point between now and publication, you should change your mind, just let me know. For now, I have prepared a document for you both to sign."

I glanced over the contract she slid over to us and read it as carefully as Mom. Dr. Steinberg really did include a clause that allowed us to back out until the day before publication. And she had to inform us of said date the moment she knew it, which, as per contract, had to be at least three weeks before actual publication.

Apparently, the paper's initial publication was set to be an online one, with the printed magazine only being distributed once a month.

After a last moment of contemplation, Mom signed it as my guardian.

"I better get out so you can begin your session," she said with an uncertain smile, handing the page back to Dr. Steinberg.

"See you in an hour," I called after her as she left.

"So, Ben," Dr. Steinberg said, crossing her legs. "Tell me about why you didn't tell your mom about the injury."

Chapter 22

I watched my phone like a hawk all day, waiting for a message from Jack that would tell me that the bowl had finally arrived. But I received nothing of the sort. Understandable, since he was most likely in school himself. I did, however, get hourly photo updates from Vivienne on how school was going. There was even a picture of her, Cindy, and Harvey having lunch together.

Once I figured that Jack should have made it home, I texted him to ask about the bowl. His answer was almost instantaneous.

Yeah, I picked it up on the way home from school. Remind me why you wanted it again?

Had he not been paying attention? Frowning, I texted back.

It's for Tara's ritual. Gotta ask her if you want details.

I didn't get a response from him after that. I figured he probably took my advice and asked Tara.

I felt relieved. We had all the components we needed to perform the ritual to transport us back to Halastaesia. To end this once and for all.

Then my phone rang with an unknown number. Hesitantly, I picked up.

"Hello?"

"Hey, champ." My dad's voice.

My shoulders relaxed instantly. I wasn't sure what I'd expected, but hearing him was immensely relieving.

"I just wanted to check how you're doing."

Somehow his voice sounded laden with heaviness. I was guessing that Mom had told him about my accident.

"I'm doing fine, Dad. Nothing to worry about."

He sighed, deeply.

"Dad?" I asked. "Are you doing okay?"

"I … Son. Ben. I just need you to know that we love you very much, your mom and I."

Okay, this conversation was taking a weird turn.

"I know that. But what's going on, Dad? I just had a little accident, it's nothing to worry about, really."

He chuckled, sadly.

"It's funny." I could hear the little smile in the corner of his mouth. "You're right here, but you feel so distant. I wish you'd just take my hand. Let me help you."

I laughed disconcertedly. "You'll just have to come home again soon. Let me beat you in a round of basketball."

The line went dead as he hung up.

Rude!

I stared at my phone for a moment. I hadn't realized how much news of my little accident might perturb him. I supposed that his constant distance to his family might weigh on him more than I ever realized. Whenever anything happened, he couldn't just drop everything and come here. Even if he could, it would still take him the better part of a day.

It wouldn't surprise me if he wished he could be around more. But he was a soldier, and as such he wasn't at liberty for that—at least not at short notice—he had to follow orders.

My time in Halastaesia had made me understand what it meant to be a soldier, a fighter. It meant bearing responsibility. Leaving didn't just mean deserting your post. It meant letting down every single one of your comrades. It meant creating a gap the enemy could exploit to turn the fight against your friends.

"Sorry, Dad," I muttered.

Wow, more guilt. That stuff was really piling up. I was beginning to wonder if I'd ever be clear of that.

Probably not.

Friday had come.

Mom and Jack's mother left early in the

morning for their trip, while Vivienne and Jack went to school for the first few periods. I headed over to his house ahead of time, bringing nothing but my sword, hoping that I could discuss the ritual with Tara and check on the preparations in general before we needed to get started.

Ringing the doorbell didn't seem to alert anyone to open up for me, so I climbed over the garden gate instead to get to the back. There, I found my three Halastaesian friends prepping a small stone circle. The bowl and crystal were out here as well.

"Hey, guys."

Phillip raised an eyebrow at me. "You've missed several days of preparation."

Ronan clapped his shoulder. "He was just scared of another beatdown," he jested and winked at me.

I grimaced and tossed him my sword. "Actually, my injuries came back and my mom found out. I didn't want to worry her any more, so I stayed home. I figured I wouldn't really be much help here anyway."

Tara, who had been placing rocks up to that point, shot up and turned to me, alarmed. "Your injuries came back? You mean the ones I healed?"

I pulled up my trouser leg to show her my bandages. Once more, she undid them, gaping at the healing wounds. She shook her head in disbelief.

"That's impossible. I healed them. I know I did!"

"Well," I said hesitantly, "they reappeared when a Corrupted One showed up in my room."

Upon their shocked looks, I recounted my little fun adventure with a Corrupted One's bite from the ground. They exchanged concerned glances.

"So they somehow reversed Tara's magic?" Phillip asked.

Ronan took a step toward me. "Have you seen any more of them since?"

"No, that was the last time. I think they might be biding their time."

"But why?"

Tara had voiced the question we were all thinking. Why bother biding their time? They didn't have anything to gain from that. Unless … Those little incidents had only been set up to scare us. To make us think the mages were further ahead than they actually were. Perhaps so we would rush things. Run into things before we were ready. To mess it up, and ruin our chance of getting to Halastaesia on time. But since I had barely told my friends about what had been happening until now, there'd been no danger of that. Perhaps that was why the random attack had stopped.

Once more, Tara healed the wounds on my legs. I needed them to be in optimal condition so I could fight and win. Though, to be frank, the painkillers were working so efficiently, that most the time I barely felt them anyway.

"So," I said then, looking from one of the Halastaesians to the next. "Once we get there, what's the plan? Do you know where we'll land?"

The guys exchanged an awkward look, and Tara sighed.

"We have no idea," she admitted. "This is our first time traveling across worlds. Well, second, I suppose. We might show up back where we left, or we could appear where you did when you first arrived. But honestly, for all I know, it could be entirely random. The only thing I am relatively certain of is that we'll get there together, like we did on the way here."

Everything she said made perfect sense to me.

"But we'll need to move fast," Phillip added. "We don't have the luxury of taking the time to dilly dally or go sightseeing. If we want to catch the mages off guard, we need to talk to my intelligence forces immediately and figure out the fastest and easiest way to infiltrate the castle quickly. Or hope that Tara's little plan works better than expected and we can actually plop right in the center of the throne room."

"What about weapons?"

I looked to Ronan to answer my question. If anyone would know the answer to this one, it would be him.

Unfortunately, he grimaced.

"I don't think we'll be able to prepare anything. If it's anything like it was for us last time, we won't be able to bring anything except for the clothes on our back and the things we're holding. Which essentially means we've got two options: Either get Tara to summon us some more swords quickly once we arrive, or hope we can grab something that's lying around."

The rumpling of his nose informed me that he liked those ideas about as much as I did. I had my sword, currently strapped to Ronan's back, and Phillip had his bow, but Tara would likely be exhausted from the ritual and might not be fast enough in summoning weapons for the other three if her plan worked and we'd land in the midst of the mages. We had to expect magical attacks to come at us instantly, really. And we'd have to deal with those somehow on top of trying to attack ourselves. God, I hoped our element of surprise worked.

Vivienne and Jack arrived after first period, blowing off the rest of the school day. We did kind of have more pressing business to attend to. Like saving two worlds from some megalomaniac mages.

We didn't talk much. Truthfully, we didn't do much more than shoot each other concerned glances. Of course Jack and Vivienne were nervous, it was their first time visiting another world. Never mind the fact that we were heading straight into battle. I couldn't deny that I was nervous, too.

Any other time I'd moved across realms, it had been sudden, unexpected. I'd never experienced this anticipation, wondering whether it would work, how it would happen, how it would feel. This was new to me, too, in a way.

As Tara waved us over to enter her stone circle, Ronan holding the crystal, Phillip holding the bowl, I nodded at Jack, and took Vivienne's hand.

I was glad they were with me for this. I was happy they would join in this adventure, that I could share Halastaesia with them. I was glad not to be alone. To not be returning from Halastaesia alone, again. Two of the most important people in my life were traveling with me. And then there were the others. My friends from another world who came here to warn me, to help me. And who had risked everything to keep me safe.

Tara knelt in the center of our circle. Closing her eyes, she began to chant in a low voice, speaking words that didn't exist, sounds that couldn't be created. Her voice echoed through time and reverberated through space. They entered every fiber of my being, making my skin tingle and crackle with energy.

Starting from her lips, a green glow spread across Tara, as though her breath itself was magical. Her hair rose up as if electrified, and from that, the green glow spread to the stone circle around us, lighting up one stone after the other, until the whole ring was alight. Then, the single glows unified, shaping a translucent hemisphere around us. Looking out of the dome was like looking through green fire. The world seemed distorted, somehow, glimmering as if it wasn't stable.

Vivienne's hand in mine began to tremble, and I squeezed it to reassure her. It would be alright.

Tara knew her magic. I'd never seen her mess up a spell. I'd only seen her create something this elaborate maybe once or twice in my entire time in Halastaesia, but nevertheless, I trusted her. I believed that she could do this, that she could bring us back.

Still, my palms were getting sweaty, and my heart rate increased. I'd be lying if I'd claimed I was calm. I was anything but.

I wasn't even sure if I should be excited, scared, or worried. So often I'd wished I could return to Halastaesia, even just visit again. Now I was getting that chance, but I doubted that I'd be able to enjoy it.

Finally, Tara ceased her chanting, and opened her eyes. Instead of irises, green flames surrounded her pupils when she turned to the crystal and bowl the other two were holding out to her. She took them both, one in each hand. The moment she began to chant anew, the crystal began to spark tiny lightning, as if the energy contained inside was too strong to be kept. Slowly, reverently, she pulled her hands together.

I held my breath, watching hypnotized as she placed the crystal into the bowl.

The moment they touched, lightning struck in the center of our circle.

For several moments, I could do little more than groan. I was in so much pain. The explosion of impact had thrown me several feet backward, knocking my back against something hard. My vision was still blotchy and blinded, while my hearing could make out little more than ringing. Vivienne's hand had been pulled from my grasp in the explosion, and I dizzily scrambled to my arms and knees to look for her.

I could only hope that wherever we'd landed wasn't enemy territory, because I was a useless, sitting duck right now. I didn't even want to imagine in what kind of state Jack and Vivienne might find themselves.

After a few moments, my senses were finally able to pick up my surroundings and I shakily rose to my feet, whipping around to see where I was.

Panic rose inside of my chest.

No.

No, this wasn't right!

It couldn't be!

I was still in Jack's garden. The stone circle was exactly where it had been mere moments ago. In fact, the entire place looked just like it had seconds earlier—no scorch marks, no smoking earth, no barrier. But something very definitive had changed.

I was alone.

Chapter 23

My mind raced as I scanned my surroundings. It couldn't be right. They'd all been here seconds ago. We'd all stood in the circle together and Tara had done something with her magic. She'd done something and it had worked … well, it had worked something.

I wiped away sweat from my upper lip with a jerky movement before ruffling through my hair.

What had happened?

Why was I still here when no one else was?

I didn't dare to focus on the terrible thought edging around my mind.

The garden was empty.

I turned to go into the house, hoping that this had just been a prank of some sort, but when I tried to open the back door, I found it locked.

Weird. I could have sworn that Jack and Vivienne had come through there only a few minutes ago, and I was pretty sure he'd never locked it after him. So I went back out to the front of the house and rang the doorbell.

No answer. Peeking in through the windows didn't get me any further, either. Once more I walked into the garden, but it was just as I'd left it. Empty.

How could this have happened?

My heart was beating like a drum, echoing in my ears. All sounds seemed to be a million yards away. As energy surged through my limbs, I sought to give them relief and let go of my inhibitions. Roaring in anger and frustration, I kicked bushes, rocks, and garden gnomes, after throwing chairs and flipping the table.

Bits of grass flew through the air, flowerpots were smashed into millions of tiny little pieces, gnomes were drowned in the pond, if they weren't brutally murdered by means of decapitation.

Eventually, my rampage through Jack's garden slowed and grinded to a halt. Breathing heavily, I dropped the garden hose I'd just been using as a whip on the innocent plant life. Then, I fell to the floor, burying my head between my knees.

They were gone.

Somehow, Tara's spell had spirited them all away, but left me behind. I was the one who was left here, even though I was the one the mages were after. And what about Vivienne and Jack? Without me there, who would look out for them? Sure, my Halastaesian friends would do their best, but they didn't know how it felt to be in Halastaesia for the first time. To suddenly experience real magic. To fight demons for the first time. How it was simultaneously terrifying and exhilarating.

And what if something happened?

What if they couldn't return, or worse?

I bit my lip, forcing my thoughts to take a different turn.

Right.

I needed to figure out what to do next.

Was there another way for me to follow them? To get to Halastaesia after all?

Briefly, for a blink of time, I considered reconstructing my previous accident. But just as quickly as the thought had occurred to me, I also waved it away.

There was no guarantee it would work. And I couldn't do that to my mom. Who knew if I'd wake up in a reasonable amount of time, or at all?

Besides, for all I knew, that was just what the mages wanted.

But there had to be another way. Somehow.

Finally accepting that there was nothing more for me to do here, I sluggishly hauled myself out of the garden, and headed home, sending Mom an unscheduled text message on the way.

Still doing fine. Love you, Ben.

Frantically thinking of places where the veil between the worlds might be thinner and somehow, magically open up a way for me to pass over to Halastaesia, only three places came to mind. Three places where I'd recently encountered Corrupted Ones: school, home, and the carnival.

Going to school was out of the question. If I showed up there now, chances were that I wouldn't be able to leave until the end of the day. The carnival was probably still restricted by the authorities, which left only my room. For now.

To be honest, it felt as though home was calling to me, as if there was a little voice in the back of my head pleading for me to come home. Incidentally, that voice sounded a lot like Mom.

But even as I inserted the key into the door, I knew it was wrong. I wouldn't find anything here. Why would I? And even if Corrupted Ones could come here, how in the world would I manage to get to Halastaesia that way? They didn't travel in a way I could mimic, magic or no.

But Tara had created a pathway before today. In the same place they had done. Perhaps the mixture, the combination of both magics could just be enough to allow me to change worlds ...

Even though I didn't believe that would bear any fruit, I had to try.

I went inside for a moment, just to grab a few things, including some rations and water in a backpack, along with a wooden practice sword that I had picked up some years ago. Then I hauled my bike out of the garage.

A little bird was fluttering inside of my chest, nervous and anxious. Scanning my surroundings constantly did little to calm my nerves. But I couldn't help expecting another Corrupted One to show up and ambush me any second now. Being the only one left in this world made me vulnerable. The perfect target.

As I pedaled down the streets, my desperation started to turn to hope.

Perhaps being the perfect target was exactly what I should do. It wasn't what I was used to from Halastaesia, but playing bait might allow my friends to put an end to all of this. Since the mages wanted me—or whatever it was I had stolen—it was likely that they'd focus their attention on me if I baited them, giving my friends the opportunity to strike unnoticed.

Elated by the thought, my legs moved even faster to carry me to the fairgrounds.

As I'd expected, it was still barred off with red tape, but at least I couldn't see any people or police vehicles.

The set up of the carnival still stood in the same spot, untouched. It looked ghostly, in the stillness of the morning, eerie in its silence. Some crows had taken up roost on the Ferris wheel, ogling down at me like bad omens as I ducked underneath the tape and slowly headed onto the carnival.

I had expected to only find an empty plot of land, since carnival folks weren't exactly known to abandon their trailers and attractions, but perhaps the police required the carnival to stay as it was for their investigation. I doubted that they believed the tale of the noxious gasses internally. Even now, walking among the wrecks, plenty of traces of the attack of the Corrupted Ones glared out at me. Granted, I knew what I was looking for in the tracks, in the gashes of cloth, in the destroyed attractions, but nevertheless, they were obvious enough that anyone willing to see them should notice.

I wandered around, peeking into stalls here and there along the way. Where had Tara, Phillip, and Ronan actually appeared? There had to be some sort of sign. Maybe something they'd dropped, maybe the earliest signs of a fight. Something.

Plenty of things had been left and lost that day. I saw purses no one had bothered to collect, paper cups that had been dropped and presumably spilled, there were even still some signs of rotting food, though most of the scraps had been claimed by the crows and other scavenging animals.

Walking around through this scene felt surreal. The incident felt simultaneously as fresh in my memory as though it had been yesterday, but just as much like several months had passed.

I paused next to the haunted house Vivienne and I had entered together. Where my world had been turned upside down once more. I'd finally convinced myself that my time in Halastaesia had been nothing more than a coma dream, that none of it had actually been real. I'd finally come to terms with it, and started to really live my life again. And then, the Corrupted One growing from the shadows had returned the truth to me.

I almost felt like I should be grateful, but it was difficult to feel any thanks when looking around the carnage they had caused.

I felt like I was the main character in a post apocalyptic movie and zombies were about to jump out and attack me.

Well, that probably wasn't that far away from the truth. Figuring the steel pipe that had been torn from one of the attractions probably served a better weapon than my wooden sword that was liable to snap at first impact, I picked it up, clutching it tightly.

Slowly, I paced in a circle.

"Yo," I shouted into the still carnival. "Mages! I'm here to give you the thing you wanted back. You should probably come and get it now."

Eyeing the shadows, keeping alert for any form of movement, I still flinched when one of the crows started to caw. And yet, the rest of the carnival remained still, dead, empty.

I was alone.

But why?

I was handing the mages a golden opportunity on a silver platter, so why weren't they taking it?

I could only think of two reasons—they were too busy dealing with my friends because the surprise attack had worked, or they simply didn't have the power to travel here just yet. Perhaps Tara's suspicion had been right, and they'd used up their energy on intimidation, siccing those two Corrupted Ones on me before.

"Helloho?" I sang. "Anybody here? I'm waiting!"

Nothing.

Kicking a stone angrily, I decided to take a walk around the place. I wasn't ready to give up. Not yet. Maybe I'd be able to find something … anything.

I started by heading into the haunted house, still and dead as I walked past the displays. No costumed part-timers jumped out at me to draw a scream from my lungs. No shadows rose from the ground to prove me right. I paused just before the exit in the same place where Vivienne had seen a Corrupted One for the first time. But nothing was waiting for me. After a few moments of quiet contemplation, I barged out again, frustrated with the situation and with myself.

My phone buzzed.

Unlocking the screen, I saw a photo of Mom and Jack's mother in terrible green facemasks smiling back at me. Huh. Somehow, I'd always thought those masks were only a movie thing, not something people actually used. I shot back a quick reply.

I don't think that look suits you. I

recommend not wearing that to work.

Her reply was almost instant.

Very funny, you jokester. Don't forget to check in with Dr. Steinberg. Love you.

Ah yes, I'd almost forgotten that we'd agreed I'd check in with Dr. Steinberg around dinner time today.

But right now wasn't the time for that. Since it didn't look like I was going to be transported to Halastaesia any time soon, I might as well wait with contacting the doc until I got home again.

I continued wandering across the carnival, heading to the Ferris wheel. Inspecting it from a distance, it looked in better shape than I remembered it being. I'd thought there'd been much more damage dealt to it by the brawl, but it stood firmly, as though the worst that had happened to it was some people panicking.

I was startled for a moment, but then I reminded myself that I'd been somewhat stressed at the time. I probably just misremembered it. After all, I'd been worried about Vivienne's safety. It wasn't like I'd spent a lot of time inspecting the damage on the device.

Moving on, I found more traces of panic. More people than I had realized had actually seen the monsters, it seemed. There were even some traces of human blood and items that had clearly been used as weapons, such as broken bottles.

I shuddered as I passed the scenes one by one.

If this was what the mages could accomplish in

a few hours at a carnival, I didn't want to know what they could do with the world as a whole. At this point, I could only pray to some otherworldly deity that my friends were beating our enemies. Because I was stuck here, helpless and useless.

Continuing my tour of the wreckage, I was astonished at how little actual proof of the Corrupted Ones I saw. At least, something that authorities might consider proof of non-humanoid creatures with giant claws and teeth attacking a carnival.

Even I would have doubted their prior presence here if I hadn't actually been fighting them.

As though they felt my uncertainty, a murder of crows took to the skies in one fluttering movement, their loud cawing almost echoing in the stillness of this place.

Startled, I looked up, and, not seeing where I was going, tripped over a stuffed lion which had used to be the prize at a dart throwing stand. I stumbled forward, dropping the steel pipe, and I'd held out my hands in front of myself to catch myself should I fall. Luckily, I regained my balance before it came to it.

When I looked up again, the world had changed.

CHAPTER 24

I was still standing in the same spot at the carnival, but I could feel the creeping sensation crawl along my spine, setting all my hairs and goosebumps to high alert. The world had become a little darker, almost as if someone had laid a filter over it.

If I hadn't noticed it already, the tingling in my fingertips would have alerted me to the fact that something was happening. Something different. Something magical.

They were coming for me.

As though they had heard my thought and taken it as their cue, shadows all around me developed into black, ash-like mist on the ground and accumulated, shapes growing and becoming more distinct by the second. Barely a moment later, they had coalesced into several fully formed Corrupted Ones surrounding me and snarling.

I didn't move. Neither did they.

Rooted to the spot, they were clearly waiting for some sort of signal from their masters. Having dropped my rod, I was left without a weapon right now.

I'd barely finished forming that concern in my head, when a flash of light blinded me.

"Well, well, well, if it isn't the mighty hero."

The voice was familiar, but I still couldn't fully recognize who it belonged to until the spots in my vision faded a moment later, revealing a person clad in a white robe. By my world's standards, it would look like a bleached friar's robe, but I knew better.

A mage.

"Hero."

Even though his voice was quiet, it oozed authority and confidence. That was nothing new. Back when I had believed them to be on the same side as me, they'd been no different. Always so certain of themselves, like they could do no wrong.

Incidentally, they'd also never bothered saying my name. Truth be told, I wasn't even sure they knew it. Though, in their defense, even I didn't think "Ben" was a very heroic name. It didn't exactly drip with charisma the same way superhero names in movies did.

"I almost feel bad for putting you against such odds." The mage gestured mildly at the Corrupted Ones around me.

I shifted my weight, making sure of my footing. "Don't underestimate me."

The mage laughed quietly. "I wouldn't dare. We've seen what you can do. But unlike in

Halastaesia, you're on your own now, so how about we even the odds just a little?"

He snapped his fingers, and with a bright light, a glowing sword rose from the ground. Of course it could be a trap. I might touch it and immediately fall under a spell. But that wasn't the mages' style. Especially when they felt so certain of their victory. He was right. I was indeed outnumbered. And my backup was in another world, which essentially meant that it was unattainable.

I wrapped my fingers around the hilt and lifted it from its invisible stand. Even in my hand it still emitted a faint, white glow, as though the blade were crafted from stardust.

The mage's grin widened, the only feature of his face that was visible from under his hood.

And then the Corrupted Ones attacked.

It wasn't like in old Kung Fu movies where they came at me neatly one after the other so I could deal with them in turn ... oh no, they launched all at once. My only benefit lay in the fact that they tried not to get in each other's way. There were eight of them, in total. One of them tried to grab me, while a second one snapped its fangs at me, and a third slashed my way with its claws. I managed to jerk back from the slash and bite in time, but I couldn't evade the grab, and the monster's talons closed around me. In a quick bout of inspiration, I struck the creature's eyes with my sword, effectively blinding and shocking it. Its grasp loosened immediately as it backed away, howling.

I didn't gain any time to rejoice in having at least temporarily immobilized one of them, because there were still seven more Corrupted Ones trying to get a piece of me. Number four and five lunged at me from two different sides, but I used the opening the first one had just created for me to sprint out of the circle of attackers. I didn't make it out unscathed, however. Number six jumped in my way, waving talons through the air, and in my attempt at leaping past it, I received three gashes on my biceps. Doing my utmost to ignore the sudden, burning sting, I used what little time I had gained to jump onto a trash can, from which I climbed onto one of the stands.

However, it appeared I wasn't the first to have thought of gaining the advantage through height. Number seven was already waiting for me up there, while number eight was in the process of climbing up on the far side. At least I only had one opponent to fight for a second.

I clutched the sword tighter in the brief moment we eyed each other up.

Then, almost as one, we both lunged forward, claws and sword ready to slash. But instead of swinging at the Corrupted One, I ran, ducked to evade its attack, and threw myself between its legs, rolling my way past and to my feet again. Coming up behind it, I used my advantage and plunged the sword into its neck.

I'd barely torn it free again when number eight was on me.

Unlike the others, it counted on distance, using its long tail to its advantage. I didn't even notice it was up on the roof already until I was whipped across the back by its spiny tail scales.

Gasping at the impact, I lost my footing for just a moment and dropped to my knees. Before I could even fully comprehend the burning pain that streaked across my back, the Corrupted One's assault continued. The force of its strike knocked the breath out of my lungs, and I dropped forward, landing on my hands.

No more.

I kicked myself off with my legs and rolled away and to my feet before I turned around.

The Corrupted One watched me carefully, swinging its tail like an impatient cat. I wasn't sure if it was just my imagination, but it seemed smarter than the ones I was used to fighting.

Slowly, it took a few steps forward, and put one claw on the sword I had dropped when it had first struck me.

Gnashing my teeth, I allowed myself to take a split second to take in the general situation. One of the other Corrupted Ones, probably number five or six—who could really tell—was climbing up on the roof as well, the others waiting just below me as if to wait for me to attempt an escape or fall.

Beyond them, the mage was watching cheerfully, having taken a seat on a busted horse of a carrousel. Its head had been completely torn off, but the mage didn't seem to mind all that much. His eyes were trained on me, his amusement clear.

Damn.

I was already panting, my heartbeat racing at formula one speeds and I'd only taken down one of the Corrupted Ones so far before losing my sword. A rookie move if ever there was one.

Maybe ... maybe I couldn't win this fight.

I couldn't give up either. That was certainly a decision that could only end in death. So the only option I had left was trying to hold out for long enough for my friends in Halastaesia to settle the score.

How exactly I was going to do that, I didn't know.

But then my gaze fell on the rusty iron rod I'd carried earlier. The Corrupted Ones had left its proximity as they'd been doing their best to tail me instead. If I could get across them, grab it, and run ... perhaps I could find a location that was more advantageous for me to fight. Dealing with this many monsters at once while they could come at me from every side wasn't going to work. I needed a narrower space, so they would be hindered not only by their size, but by one another.

Two Corrupted Ones had made it onto the roof

now.

Where to run?

The answer came to me like a flash of lightning.

Where I'd beaten my first Corrupted One on Earth. The space had provided the perfect advantage for me. They could easily take that advantage away from me, by breaking down the setting, but I didn't believe that they would. I didn't expect they would be smart enough, and the mage seemed to be enjoying the show too much to interfere.

Clinging on to that hope, I jumped off the roof, doing my best to jump far enough to land behind the waiting Corrupted Ones on the ground and roll to my feet into a run. I ducked briefly to pick up the rod without so much as slowing down in my sprint.

I didn't look back. They'd be following me all right.

I also knew they were faster than me.

If I slowed down even the tiniest bit, they'd bite my head off. Literally.

I could hear the scurrying and scratching of their claws along the ground as they gained on me.

Still, I reached the haunted house unscathed. The moment before I ducked inside, I dared to shoot one last glance back after all and saw ... nothing. I'd already entered the tunnel when I realized and peeked back out. Nothing. The

Corrupted Ones were nowhere in sight.

"What?" The quiet word escaped my lips before I could stop myself.

I flinched at the sound, scolding myself for making noise, possibly revealing myself.

But nothing happened.

Nothing disturbed the stillness of the carnival, except my own rapid breathing.

What in the world was going on? How had the Corrupted Ones just … vanished? I'd heard them tailing me until just a moment before, hadn't I? But they weren't here now. In fact, there wasn't the slightest trace of them anywhere to be seen.

I stepped out fully, at a loss. I knew they couldn't just vanish. They didn't have teleportation abilities and it didn't exactly seem in the mage's best interest to magic them away at this point.

So what had happened?

I surveyed the carnival slowly, confused and startled.

There could only be one answer to this question. At least it was the only one that came to my mind.

My friends must have done it. They must have beaten the mages.

Even though I couldn't explain it any other way, I couldn't fully believe it yet. First, I needed to check it with my own two eyes.

Clutching the iron rod even tighter, I made my

way back to where I had left the mage, while keeping a constant watchful eye on my surroundings. I took my time, because I didn't want to rush into an ambush, or miss any signs along the way.

When I got there, the carrousel was empty. The mage nowhere in sight.

My friends had done it.

Endorphins rushed through my body, and I sank against a wall, finally allowing myself to relax just a little.

They'd done it. It was over.

The Corrupted Ones would never appear in this world again.

The mages would never get the chance to harm either Halastaesia or Earth ever again. It was over.

"This world of yours, it's quite intriguing."

The voice at my back let shivers run down my spine, and instantly, all tension returned to my muscles.

Whirling around, I held out the rod in front of me, ready to attack or defend. The mage smirked at me.

I'd been wrong. Celebrated too soon. Far too soon. If he'd wanted to, he could have killed me right then and there. My guard had been completely lowered.

So why hadn't he?

"We've been watching you for a while, hero. And what we've seen of your world in the process … Well, it's beyond our wildest dreams. You understand that we need it, don't you?"

He was too far away to hit with my rod. And with his magic, he was at an advantage at this distance. I wouldn't be able to close the gap quickly enough. But for some reason, he seemed intent on having a chat.

I only glared at him in response.

He chuckled quietly. "Look, we only need to regain your essence. The essence of the hero. Once we have that, we can cross over and make this world a better place. You need the help, you know. Look at how much criminality goes on here. How much hunger this world suffers while some stuff their faces and throw the rest away. How selfish your people are. You as well. You're a thief, you realize that, don't you?" His gaze hardened. "You took something that didn't belong to you. And we'd like it returned to us now."

Chapter 25

"You had the chance to kill me just now." I shifted my weight, ready to try climbing the trailer where I'd left the sword. Without it, I didn't stand a chance. "Why didn't you?"

"You're no use to us dead." The mage laughed.

Before I could respond, the phone in my pocket started buzzing. Probably Mom since I hadn't sent her an update yet. Possibly missed a few texts. I tried to ignore it, but the mage pleasantly nodded at my pocket.

"You better take that," he said. "I have a feeling it's important."

Slowly, without lifting my eyes from him, I reached into my pocket to fish out my phone.

I lifted it to my ear and picked up. "Hello?"

The mage, as if to give me privacy for my phone call, turned his back to me. I decided to use this opportunity to start climbing the trailer while pinning my phone between my shoulder and ear.

"Hey, bud."

I froze in place. "Jack?"

But how?

If I'd known I could phone him in Halastaesia, I would have done that hours ago!

With a glance at the mage, I continued my ascent.

"How are things over there?" I asked, doing my best to sound as nonchalant as possible, since the mage was almost certainly listening in on my side of the conversation. Hard not to overhear, anyway.

Jack sighed. Heavily. "Nothing's the same without you."

What a weird thing to say. It wasn't like he'd ever experienced Halastaesia *with* me.

"I'm still fighting, but I don't have my rival anymore. Kinda sucks, you know?"

"I'm fighting, too," I said, reaching the top of the trailer. "But we'll be done soon, right? Is Vivi okay?"

"Just … come back to us soon, 'kay? Promise me."

"You're the ones who need to come back to me, you know. But yeah. We'll be back together soon. Promise."

The call was cut off. I stared at the screen for a moment, puzzled by the conversation I'd just had. At the fact that I'd been able to even *have* this conversation.

Then, pocketing the phone once more, I picked up the sword, and jumped down from the trailer again.

Jack didn't sound like he had a lot of hope.

He'd sounded like he expected that we wouldn't see each other again. Things must have turned out worse than expected over there. I gulped. I didn't even want to imagine what that truly meant.

"How is your friend doing?" the mage asked, smiling wickedly.

"He's fine," I growled, clutching the sword tighter. What was the best way to finish this?

"Oh?" He raised his eyebrows. "What about the other one?"

I hesitated. "Who?"

Then I heard it. Soft crying at the edge of my hearing. It didn't have a distinctive source or direction, it was like it was being broadcast directly into my mind. And I recognized it instantly.

I lunged forward, sword ready to strike.

"What did you do to her?"

The mage evaded my attack easily, sidestepping and tripping me up so I fell face first onto the floor.

I quickly jumped to my feet again, wiping the dirt from the corner of my mouth with my shoulder.

"Oh, nothing at all. The real question is what you've done to them."

"Where is Vivi?" I growled, narrowing my eyes at the mage.

He shrugged and laughed. "You can end this right now, you know. All you have to do is give up your essence to me."

There was only one way out.

Sorry, Mom. Sorry, Dad. Sorry, Jack and Vivi. I couldn't think of another way to end this.

They said I was no use to them dead. Which meant that they wouldn't be able to access the hero's essence if I died. It would go with me.

Taking a deep breath, I raised my hands, and plunged the sword into my own chest.

There was no darkness or light. All I saw was flashes of the faces of my loved ones. My parents, Jack, Vivi, Harvey. Even Dr. Steinberg. The Halastaesians.

And then, the faces I swam in slowly faded and gave way to a sterile, white ceiling.

My head was still fuzzy. I wasn't even sure I was awake. This seemed like it could very well be a dream. Everything was just a little hazy. Just a little too bright. Noises were all dull and yet startlingly loud.

I blinked.

My surroundings didn't change. This was familiar somehow.

My body didn't hurt where I'd expect it to ache. My throat was sore though. I tilted my head slowly to find a machine recording something, and an IV drip that led straight into my arm.

Hospital. I was in a hospital.

The door burst open, and a nurse rushed in. She almost squeaked when our eyes met. "You're awake!"

I tried to answer, but my tongue was too heavy to move. Instead, I blinked.

"It's alright." She smiled. "Don't strain yourself. Do you remember what happened? Blink twice for yes."

I strained my mind. I wasn't sure. Some disjointed memories washed over me, but nothing coherent came to mind. The nurse waited for a moment, but when I didn't blink, she nodded.

"Alright, I understand. Do you know who you are?"

Yes. I was Ben. I knew that much.

I blinked twice.

She beamed at me.

"Excellent! Just hang on here for a minute and try to relax. I'll be right back and then we can get that tube out of your mouth, okay?"

I blinked twice.

This was very familiar. Perhaps I'd seen a scene like this in a TV show sometime.

The nurse left, and I closed my eyes.

After what seemed like no more than about thirty seconds, the nurse returned, followed by a doctor, distinctly recognizable like all doctors by the open white coat and the obligatory stethoscope around his neck. He sat down on a stool beside my bed, while the nurse busied herself with getting me unhooked from the various apparatuses, starting with the tube that went down my throat.

The removal of it actually hurt, and I found myself almost throwing up.

"Here, drink this, it might soothe you a little."

The doctor handed me a lukewarm cup of what I could only assume to be tea. I took a gulp, and instantly tasted nothing except the sweetness of honey as it washed down my throat. Swallowing hurt, but he was right, the honey soothed me at least a little.

"So, Ben," the doctor said, "I'd like you to follow this pen with your eyes, okay?"

He took his pen from his coat pocket and moved it from side to side in front of my face at first, then back and forward. After he finished that little test, he shone a light in my eye and took a close look. Then he asked me some arbitrary questions, like if I knew the date I was born, if I knew my parents' names, and so on. I whispered the answers whenever I could, unable to speak due to my hurting throat.

After a while, the doctor seemed satisfied, and left the nurse to do the rest of my unhooking. When she was done, the only thing that remained attached to me was the IV.

"Your parents will be right by," she said cheerfully. "We made sure to call them the moment you were awake."

I nodded gratefully.

She left, leaving me with a few minutes to myself for the first time since waking up.

I spent this time trying to collect myself and my thoughts.

I was exhausted.

What had happened? Why was I here? I couldn't find any injuries on my body, at least no obvious, unhealed ones. However, I did find a ring in my left hand. Somehow, I'd been clutching it while asleep.

Inspecting it, suddenly memories came flooding back to me. My time in Halastaesia, first. Then my return home. Talking to Dr. Steinberg, dating Vivienne, falling out with Harvey, meeting my Halastaesian friends again, and then, the carnival. My rendezvous with the mage. When I took my own life. Or so I'd thought.

What had happened? Had Jack and Vivienne return yet? Had they succeeded? Or maybe … had my failed suicide attempt allowed the mages to take a hold of the essence they so sorely sought?

Riled up, I tried to leave the bed, hoping to find answers elsewhere, outside perhaps, maybe find someone with a phone so I could call or message Jack. But my limbs were weak, as though the muscles had been still for too long … again. How long? How much time had passed this time?

Before I could contemplate the question for too long, the door opened once again, and my parents stormed in. Mom burst into tears when seeing me awake. Even Dad had tears in his eyes. Like last time, deep, dark shadows darkened their eyes.

Tears entered my eyes, too.

"I'm sorry," I whispered hoarsely. "I'm so sorry."

Mom threw her arms around me, sobbing into my clavicle. I awkwardly stroked her back. To think I'd actually put her through this twice ... I really was a horrible son. But I hadn't seen another way out. No other way to protect everyone important to me, like her.

Dad joined the embrace, putting his arms around both of us.

"I'm sorry," I repeated.

Finally, after what seemed like hours, they released me, though their tears didn't stop. Neither did mine.

Still, there was something else I needed to find out. Something that was more important to me than anything.

"Where are Jack and Vivi? Are they okay?" I whispered.

I had to repeat my words twice for my parents to actually understand what I was asking. They exchanged a concerned glance in silence.

"Don't you worry about that now. Just rest up,

okay?" Dad said, tilting his head as he watched me, a firmness in his eyes that betrayed him.

My body grew cold.

What was with their reaction? Had they never returned from Halastaesia? Were they missing still?

"I was fighting," I blabbered hoarsely. "They were fighting as well, in another world."

I touched my chest, where my stab wound should be. Through the gown, I couldn't feel a bandage nor a wound. Nothing. I couldn't even feel a scar. I rubbed it frantically, trying to find any sign but found nothing.

My head grew dizzy as my hands began to tremble.

"Maybe …" Mom looked at Dad as if to seek his support.

He stepped in immediately, placing a reassuring hand on her shoulder.

"Maybe you dreamed something? The doctor said that coma dreams can be so convincing that they seem like real life …" She trailed off.

I stared at her, her words from last time echoing in my head. Words so incredibly similar it couldn't be coincidence.

My mind was once more reeling with confusion and fear.

It had to be real. It had to be.

Wasn't it?

Had I just awoken from one very long, convoluted dream I'd convinced myself of?

Even looking down at the ring in my hand, I was at a loss about what to believe.

"What happened?"

Mom stroked my forehead gently. "Oh, honey, there was an incident by the fairgrounds …"

THE END

Snowy Wings Publishing

Snowy Wings Publishing is an independent, author-run publisher of Middle Grade and Young Adult fiction. We were founded in 2016 by a diverse group of authors from a variety of publishing backgrounds—from traditionally-published authors looking to breathe new life into old works or revitalize their careers by taking control of their new series, to veteran indie authors wanting to share their expertise in a group environment and branch into markets previously accessible only in traditional spheres.

Our Mission
We are an UN-traditional publisher focused on providing authors with a team that supports and boosts each other, while also enabling each author flexibility and independence. In a time when the publishing industry is in a constant state of flux, we strive to chart our own course and find a new way that unites traditional and independent publishing to bring our works to all readers, whether they be committed Kindle owners, print book hoarders, or library lovers.

MORE BY JANINA FRANCK

Short Stories

The Weight of Time (*A Touch of Magic, 2019*)
A Spark in Space (*A Touch of Magic, 2019*)
Override (*Brave New Girls: Girls who Tech and Tinker, 2020*)
Káto Kósmos (*Sing, Goddess!, 2021*)
The Wizard's Bride (*Space Bound, 2021*)
Midnight Train (*Beyond, 2022*)
Tribute (*Hope Riot, 2022*)
Scrapyard Witch (*Brave New Girls: Girls who Engineer and Explore, 2023*)
The Night I Died (*Into the Dark Wood, 2023*)
Runaway Renegade (*Magic Under The Big Top, 2024*)

Novels

The Chronicles of the Bat
        Captain Black Shadow (*2016*)
        White Devil (*2019*)
        Sand and Snow (*2020*)

A Spark in Space: A Space Witch Novel (*2021*)

Devil Deal (*2022*)

Milton Keynes UK
Ingram Content Group UK Ltd.
UKHW030620061024
449204UK00001B/19